ONCE UPON A TIME
Regina Rising

Regina Rising

By Wendy Toliver

Based on the ABC Television series created by
Edward Kitsis & Adam Horowitz

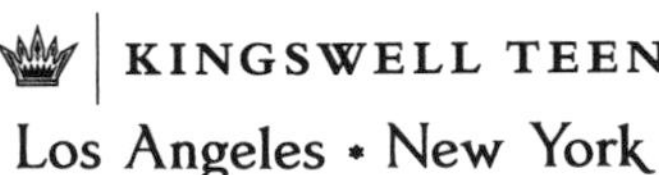

Los Angeles • New York

For information address Kingswell Teen,
1101 Flower Street, Glendale, California 91201.

Editorial Director: Wendy Lefkon
Executive Editor: Laura Hopper
Cover designed by Julie Rose

ISBN 978-1-4847-8776-2
FAC-020093-17069

Printed in the United States of America
First Hardcover Edition, April 2017
10 9 8 7 6 5 4 3 2 1

www.disneybooks.com

THIS LABEL APPLIES TO TEXT STOCK

This book is dedicated to
believers in magic and happy endings.

Regina Rising

By Wendy Toliver

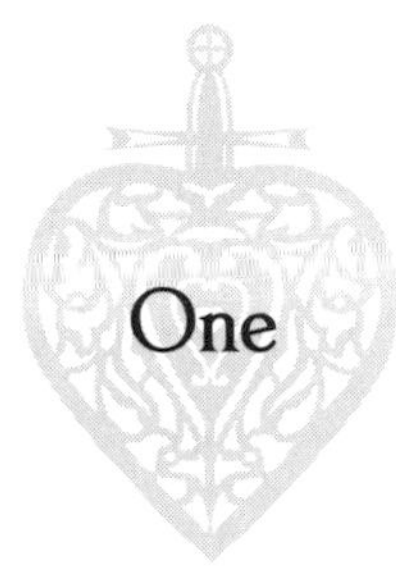

One

Friday, May 5

The bolt slammed into its brackets with a terrible bang. Cowering against the wall, I clutched my chest as if trying to keep my heart from bursting right out.

"You will stay in your room until I grant you permission to come out." My mother's voice reverberated from the bottom of the staircase to the arched ceiling and vast walls of the hallway. "Do you hear me?"

Though I couldn't see her, I pictured her standing on the landing, arms crossed and head tilted, as still as a statue—except for the plumes of residual purple smoke coming from her fingertips.

I wished she would have tromped up the stairs and locked the door with her own two hands, instead of using magic. However, subtlety was not in her nature.

"Answer me, Regina."

"Yes, Mother," I said.

I heard a faint pattering noise, but I couldn't tell if it was my mother's high heels tapping on the tiles as she walked away, or the bolt on the outside of my bedroom door trying to settle into place after having suffered such a blow.

I hung up my riding jacket and peeled off my boots. I had no idea how long I'd be imprisoned in my room, so I figured I might as well be comfortable. Heaving out a gust of air, I slid down the wall until I was seated on the rug. I'd always admired the rug my father had brought home for me from one of his many trips. Not only did it protect me from the hard, chilly floor beneath, but it also kept me amused. Growing up, I'd spent countless hours lying on my belly, letting my imagination run rampant with the adventures I could have with all the trees, flowers, and animals woven into it, as if they were real.

With the tip of my finger, I traced along the familiar scene, from the pond where frogs floated on lily pads to the stream teeming with fish, pausing when I reached the green snake coiled up on its bank.

September, ten years earlier

"Come, child," my father urged when he spied me peeking into his smoking room. I wiped my eyes on the cuff of my blouse, hoping he hadn't spotted the tears. My mother and I had gone to town, and a pair of little girls had invited me to play marbles. My mother had scooted me past before I'd even been able to answer, and when I'd begged her to let me play one little game, she'd said, "We have more important things to do." Only I couldn't think of a single thing we'd done that afternoon that was important at all.

My father finished cutting an apple and placed the slices on a plate beside his favorite chair. It was autumn, the best season of the entire year, and the orchard was bursting with beautiful red fruit.

"I have a story for you." He patted his knee and I hopped onto his lap. "Once there was an old man," he began.

"As old as you, Daddy?" I asked, pulling playfully on his beard. Unlike Mother, he never seemed to mind when I interrupted. He used the break to hand me a slice of apple.

"Even older, if you can believe it."

"Oh, I can believe it if I try *really* hard," I teased him as I relished the crispy, sweet fruit.

"Well, that's good to know," he said with a chuckle. I snuggled up to his velvety-soft vest as he continued his story. "The old man loved having his breakfast beside a beautiful gurgling brook. The animals who made their homes near the brook looked forward to his daily visit, for he always had a song to sing and brought plenty of food to share. One morning, a green snake slithered over to the old man's basket. The birds took to the air, the squirrels and rabbits and foxes scurried off—even the fish swam downstream, safely out of the snake's reach.

"'Why are you still here, old man?' the snake asked. 'Are your eyes too old to see I'm a poisonous snake?'

"'My bones might creak, my skin might be wrinkled, but there is nothing wrong with my eyes,' replied the man. He then reached into his basket and held a piece of bread before the deadly serpent.

"The snake smiled slyly at the old man as his venomous fangs sank through the bread and deep into the man's palm.

"As the snake glided away, the man jumped up as best he could on his old legs and soaked his hand in the cool waters of the brook, hoping to get relief from the pain. Soon enough, a fish spotted his wounded hand and, though the man thought it was just the waters lapping at him, sucked and spat the poison out, leaving the man to live another day.

"The following morning, the old man returned to the brook with his basket of food. As had happened the previous day, the man offered the snake some bread. Again, the snake bit him. The man shuffled to the brook and dipped his throbbing hand into the water, where another fish sucked out the poison and saved his life.

"On the third morning, the snake said to the old man, 'I do not know how you're still alive, but even more perplexing is why you keep feeding me when you know I'll bite you. I've done it before and I'll do it again. It's in my nature. It's what I do.'

"The man pondered this for a moment before reaching in his basket. 'Because,' he said, holding out a piece of bread for the snake, 'this is what *I* do.'"

I waited for my father to continue, but he just sat there, smiling down at me. "Is that it?" I asked.

"That's the end of the story," he confirmed.

"But I don't understand it."

His smile deepened and his eyes twinkled. "Someday, my child, you will."

Friday, May 5

A knock on the door startled me. It had only been a little over an hour since my mother had locked me in my room. Fearing the worst, I clambered to my feet. Wood scraped against wood. The bolt had been lifted.

I hated what I'd become, a pitiful creature who cowered when it came to my mother. For once, I wanted to have the courage to stand up to her. Alas, as long as she used her magic, she would always have the upper hand.

"Come in, Mother. Again, I'm very sorry."

To my relief, it was my father. "Actually, it's me," he said. He entered, and with him came the sweet, earthy aroma of tobacco. He looked dapper in his scarlet coat, beige breeches, and knee-high riding boots. "Your mother said you may come down for tea now. She also wanted me to tell you your horse is in the stables, and Jesse is seeing to him as we speak."

"Thank you, Daddy," I said as I brushed the wrinkles out of my blouse. I hoped he would ask what I'd done to deserve being locked in my room, but he did not. To be honest, I wasn't surprised. He seldom inserted himself between my mother and me, and I oftentimes wondered if he was afraid of her, too. "I'm surprised she's granting me my freedom so quickly this time."

He blotted his forehead with his handkerchief and then tucked it into his breast pocket. "Your mother's heart is in the right place. She only wants what is best for you, my child."

Instead of meeting his gaze, I pulled open the drapes and peered out the window. The spring rains had given the hills a surreal lushness—a shade of green that rivaled the brightest of emeralds. I could only imagine how beautiful the flowers in the royal gardens looked.

"How was the hunt?" I asked. "You went with Giles this morning, isn't that correct?" Giles Spencer was our nearest neighbor, as well as the royal doctor.

"The foxes hoodwinked us again," my father confessed. "Since today is the final day of the hunting season, I'm afraid we'll have to wait until November to salvage our reputations."

"Giles's *hunting* reputation isn't the one I would worry about, if I were him," I said, and when my father sighed, I instantly regretted my insensitivity. He was my father's friend, so I should've done better to tolerate him, even if he had been found passed out in some farmer's chicken coop the previous Saturday night.

"Since his wife and baby passed away, he isn't the same man. But when you've been friends for as long as we have, well, we stick together through all the ups and downs, the highs and lows, the good and the bad, the thick and thin. . . ."

I smiled at him as he blathered on, but deep inside I felt a pang of jealousy. Sure, I was sometimes bitter that my father chose to spend his mornings foxhunting with Giles rather than riding horses with me, but that wasn't it. It was something about the reverence with which he spoke about Giles, the way my father came to his defense without hesitation. It made me yearn for that kind of friendship myself.

My father cleared his throat, making his Adam's apple bob against his cravat. "You should hurry and change, child. Your mother is waiting."

"Is something wrong with what I'm wearing?" I gave myself a quick once-over in the mirror. The day before

I'd shown up for tea with grass stains on my hemline, and with a flick of her wrist, my mother had used her magic to change me into a clean and starched dress, glaring at me as she did so.

On second thought, perhaps I should quickly swap my riding pants and blouse for a frock straight from the laundress, just to be sure.

"A guest will be joining you," he said.

I turned back around to face him. "Really? Who?"

He winked at me. "It's a surprise. Now get ready, and I'll be waiting to take you down," he said and backed out of my room, softly closing the door. I heard him whistling a jolly little tune out in the hall.

I slipped into a simple yet pretty dress and ran a brush through my long black hair. Before leaving my room, I checked my appearance in the mirror once more, wondering again who my mother had invited to tea. I knew better than to get my hopes up that it would be somebody I'd actually *want* to meet. Knowing my mother, I'd find her sitting across from the most pitiful old maid she could dig up: a threat to show me what would become of me if I didn't begin taking her quest for me to marry a royal prince or king seriously. She'd even christened me with a name that meant "queen." I heard her voice in my mind, saying it for the thousandth time: "I named you Regina, for one day, you shall be queen."

When I opened the door, my father nodded his approval of my attire. I followed him down the stairs. We passed my parents' wedding portrait, a life-sized rendering that proved they'd made a striking couple when they were young. I paused to study their faces, something I often found myself doing. When I was a little girl, I'd seen in their eyes the look of true love—something I wished I, too, would find someday. Now that I was sixteen, however, I saw something more hidden deep in their expressions. If the artist had authentically captured what they'd been thinking that day, I'd say as a young prince, my father had appeared dutiful and proud, and as the newly crowned princess, my mother had had a triumphant glimmer in her eye.

My father had kept walking while I'd paused. Although he was balding and had thickened around his midriff in the seventeen years since he'd posed for his wedding portrait, I still thought him to be a handsome man. I took the stairs as quickly as possible to catch up with him. At the bottom, I accepted his elbow and he dutifully escorted me to the drawing room and then dismissed himself. Before entering, I took a calming breath, hoping my mother's mood had improved.

Two

My mother sat at the head of the table, staring at her reflection in a silver spoon. She was impeccably dressed in a white blouse and a fitted midnight-blue skirt. Her ears, chest, wrists, and fingers dripped with some of the finest jewels in the kingdom. "It's about time you graced us with your attendance, Regina." She placed the spoon on the lacy tablecloth. "We were about to start without you."

I winced, weighing whether it would have pleased her had I been on time, but in my riding clothes. In the conclusion of my brief inner debate, I figured she would not have been satisfied no matter what I had done.

Our guest, who until then had her back to me, promptly scooted out her chair with a dreadful screech. She stood and gave me a little curtsy as I entered the sunlit room. I was happy to see she was not a pitiful old maid. She appeared to be about my age, only taller and thinner. Her flaxen hair twisted and swirled around the crown of her head, feeding into an off-center bun at the nape of her neck. The style was fashionable enough, yet some tendrils were seemingly too stubborn to remain smoothed in place and instead floated around her head like silken spiderwebs. Her deep-green dress was plain and ill fitting, but I remembered the one I'd chosen to wear left little to boast about, either. When she finally lifted her gaze to mine, I almost gasped; her eyes were as clear and blue as my mother's best sapphire earrings. I forced myself to blink so she wouldn't think I was gawking.

"I'm sorry to have kept you waiting," I said, hoping to placate my punctuality-devoted mother. As I settled into my chair, I was pleasantly surprised that my view of my mother was obscured. In place of the usual centerpiece towered an elegant, albeit cumbersome, arrangement of orchids.

While Rainy, our faithful servant, bustled about, pouring tea and making sure the three of us had everything we could possibly need—including several spoonfuls of honey for our guest—my mother commenced the introductions. "Regina, this is Claire Fairchild. She is Giles's niece, and she's come to live with him for the season. It's a very fortuitous arrangement, as she's only a year older than you and is eager for companionship. Isn't that so, Claire?"

Claire nodded eagerly. "It's my pleasure to meet you, Regina. Your mother has told me such wonderful things about you." I'd never known my mother to say anything even vaguely "wonderful" about me to anyone. Well, anyone other than a prospective husband for me, which was always a gentleman with a strong stream of royal blood pumping through his veins.

I pondered that as I stirred two lumps of sugar into

my tea. "I never knew Giles had a niece," I said, "and Mother has never mentioned you until this very moment." As soon as the sugar dissolved, I took a quick sip, only to burn my tongue.

My mother slid the orchids out of the way, leaving the vase teetering on the edge of the table. I held my breath, fearing that at any second, it would topple and smash into bits on the gray floor tiles. She was seemingly too busy shooting me the evil eye—no doubt in response to my less than noble behavior—to notice the foreseeable calamity.

However, Claire obviously noticed, and she reached across the table to rescue the orchids before they had the chance to fall. When I met Claire's striking blue gaze, the strangest thing happened. We smiled at each other, at the exact same time.

"I'm very glad you were able to join us today, Claire," I added. Although I needed to say something polite to try and keep my mother from exploding, I actually meant what I'd said. "I am pleased to make your acquaintance."

To my relief, my mother seemed satiated, and the side of her mouth twitched into an almost-smile.

"Thank you, Regina. It's nice to be here," Claire said. "And thank you, Your Highness," she said to my mother.

My mother nodded benevolently. "You may call me Cora."

The three of us lifted our teacups and sipped, and as the moments marched along, I found my tea cooling to a more comfortable drinking temperature and my heart warming to my newest neighbor.

"Cora happened to stop in my ma's tavern when she was passing through Port Bennett, and when she mentioned her estate was located just beneath King Leopold and Queen Eva's castle, my ma told her that her brother lived there, too," Claire said as Rainy poured her more tea. Although my mother had given our guest permission to call her by her first name, it surprised me she was so comfortable doing so. Surprised and intrigued me. "She told my ma it's a wonderful place for a young, unmarried lady to find a suitable husband. It was music to her ears, as you can only imagine the sort of fellows who're drawn to a port town."

As Claire spoke, I grinned to myself, picturing the rogues who undoubtedly haunted a place like that: bandits with skilled hands and wild eyes; pirates and buccaneers with long hair and tattoos; boisterous and stinking men, unshaven and undignified, full of rum and spine-tingling tales. Maybe, if I was lucky, I would get to go there someday and hear the tales for myself. "Oh, I can only imagine," I piped up, lifting my upper lip to feign my disgust at the very existence of such men.

I wondered if the ring Claire wore on a silver chain around her neck—a garish, masculine ring, designed to look like a dragon claw curving possessively around a large dark-red stone—was a token from such a scoundrel. I was dying to know, but I'd have to wait for another time to ask, a rare moment when my mother wasn't breathing down my neck.

"Cora generously offered to give me a ride," Claire continued, "and it was decided I would spend the warmer months at my uncle's estate."

"It was no trouble at all," my mother said. "Imagine my surprise when I realized her uncle was Giles Spencer."

I highly doubted Giles would have offered to take in his niece of his own volition. Yet, as my mother was the one behind it, it was no surprise he'd agreed, if only for the sake of getting another feather in his cap, so to speak.

"Naturally, given Giles's misfortune with his own family, he was delighted to have the opportunity to get to know his next of kin," my mother said, filling me with guilt for my previous misgivings.

Solomon, a servant as cold and stony as a statue, with skin almost as gray as one, appeared at our table. "Your Highness, a messenger came by with this." He placed a scroll before my mother and rigidly backed away. I was surprised he'd dared interrupt our tea, but a cursory glance at the scroll showed it was of a fine parchment, and the wax seal bore the initial L. L, as in Leopold.

My mother unrolled the message and read aloud: "'His Majesty King Leopold and Her Majesty Queen Eva request your presence at a royal ball to celebrate the victorious end to the Ogre Wars.'" She tapped her fingernail on the parchment. "The end of the wars," she said with a little laugh. "Now, that's presumptuous."

"Don't be such a pessimist, Mother," I chided her. "Aren't you happy? Our first party invitation of the season, and it's at the royal castle."

"Indeed," she said. "And you two girls will be the belles of the ball, I'm quite certain."

"Only because you're already married, Cora," Claire said.

"My, oh my, what a sweet thing to say. I guess all the honey Rainy put in your tea is paying off," my mother quipped. Humbleness wasn't her best quality, and whenever someone paid her a compliment, it seemed to always fall a little short of what she wanted to hear.

"The tea is delicious, I meant to make mention of it sooner. Not bitter in the least, like the sort I'm used to." Our guest absently fingered the ring she wore on her necklace. "And to think, I, Claire Fairchild, will be going to the royal ball! Oh, I've always wanted to meet Queen Eva in person. I've heard so many wonderful things about the benevolent ruler. My uncle said she was the portrait of grace."

"Interesting you should mention Eva. . . ." My mother shooed Rainy and her teapot away, and I braced myself for her to say something truly blasphemous about the queen. While my mother was dreadful at being humble, she was an expert at being bitter. "You see, if it weren't for our benevolent ruler," she said, twisting the emerald and diamond ring on her fourth finger, "I would never have wed Regina's father."

Claire's eyes widened. "Really?"

"It's true," I said. "Now, Mother, I'm sure you have important matters to tend to."

"Oh, but I love a good romantic story," Claire said. "Please, Cora, continue."

I blew a stream of air up my forehead, wishing we could declare teatime over before my mother told her story. Alas, it was too late. Our guest had been successfully enticed, and my mother was more than happy to oblige.

"Very well," my mother said, placing her hands one

upon the other on the tabletop. "One day, I was delivering flour to King Xavier's castle for my father, the miller. Eva, who at the time was a princess of the northern kingdom, happened to be there visiting. I was making my way to the kitchen with the bags of flour when she tripped me, and she began complaining that my 'clumsiness' had ruined her shoes."

"I don't understand. Why would she trip you?" Claire blinked. "It doesn't seem like civil, let alone *royal*, behavior, if you ask me."

I wondered if my mother would chastise Claire for having interrupted, but instead, she merely threw back her head and laughed. "Oh, Claire, you little lamb. You'd be surprised the sort of debauchery that goes on within castle walls. And," she added in a whisper loud enough for Rainy to hear beyond the wall, "I must confess, I've contributed my fair share."

"Queen Eva actually has a valid reason for despising my mother," I told Claire, trying to push forward through the embarrassment of my mother's previous admission.

"Regina is correct," my mother said. "If I can trust you with a secret, I will tell you."

"Of course," Claire agreed. "I'm good at keeping secrets."

"You see, before that fateful day Eva publicly humiliated me, through no fault of my own, Leopold had fallen in love with me. He wanted to marry me. The problem was, he'd been engaged to Princess Eva since birth."

"But they're married now, so what happened?"

"Let's say for time's sake that it didn't work out between Leopold and me, and since Eva never left him, even after he'd professed his love for me," she said, dipping her voice in a way that made it clear she found the woman pathetic, "the two of them picked up where they'd left off."

"What did you do after Eva tripped you?" Claire prompted, sitting on the edge of her chair.

"King Xavier commanded me to kneel and apologize to her." Consumed with the memory, my mother's eyes blazed with fury.

It might have been my mind playing tricks on me, but it felt like the temperature in the room dropped. Claire rubbed her arms as if she'd caught a sudden chill, too.

"As luck would have it," my mother continued, "the king was hosting a masquerade ball so his son could choose his bride."

"His son is Prince Henry, my father," I interjected, although everybody in the Enchanted Forest—and I'd wager even those living way out in Port Bennett—knew that.

"I showed up to the ball uninvited, and when the king threatened me, I told him I could save his kingdom by spinning straw into gold," my mother said. "Of course, that kind of magic seemed impossible to him, so he put me to the test. He locked me in the tower, and I had to spin a roomful of straw into gold. If I succeeded, I would be married to the prince. If I failed, I would be executed. I'm living proof it *is* possible, and shortly thereafter, I had the supreme pleasure of looking King Xavier in the eye while I said 'I do' to his son."

Claire's blue eyes gleamed as my mother finished.

"I've never met somebody who can spin straw into gold. That's a fascinating story." For a moment or two, she sat in silence, absently dunking a biscuit into her tea. I guessed she was probably picturing my mother's magical feat in her mind. "Goodness, these biscuits are delectable. Did you bake them yourself, Cora?"

I shuddered at the thought of my mother cooking anything at all. She wouldn't be caught dead doing something as banal or beneath her as baking.

My mother laughed heartily. "Goodness, no. A sweet old lady came by on her way to the castle, peddling her baked goods. I think she called herself Granny Lucas."

"Well, then my sincerest compliments to you for having the good sense to buy them," Claire said.

I wasn't sure how I felt about Claire complimenting my mother so often, and the way she hung on to my mother's every word. Although I would be fooling myself if I claimed I never stroked my mother's ego. Mostly, I did it to win her approval. It seemed nothing I ever did worked to that end—at least, not for long.

I reached for the biscuits, but my mother slapped

my hand. "You've had enough, Regina," she said, almost sweetly.

"I've only had one. I'd like another." I sounded like a little girl, and I hated myself for it.

My mother placed her palm on King Leopold and Queen Eva's invitation, flattening and smoothing it into the table, as its edges had begun rolling back up. "It's officially party season, my dear daughter. If you're to become queen, you'd best stay away from baked goods."

I could feel my blood begin to boil. I wished I were able to say I couldn't believe my mother would say such a thing, but I could. I hated that she'd said it in front of someone with whom I might like to become friends. Under the table, I twisted my hands together until they began to ache.

"Forgive me, Cora, but your daughter is one of the fairest young ladies I've ever seen. Any man—royal or not—would be lucky to have her as his bride." Claire popped the last bite of her biscuit into her mouth. Though her hands trembled, the girl somehow managed to look my mother straight in the eyes.

A strange sensation flooded my stomach. On one hand, I wanted to leap up from my chair and hug Claire. On the other, I felt nauseated as I waited to see how my mother would react. Never before had somebody stuck out her neck for me.

As I held my breath, my mother's back stiffened and the left side of her mouth rose. "Claire, you're quite correct."

At that very moment, I had a good feeling about the blond girl who sat at my right hand. I finished the last drops of my tea, thinking how fortunate I would be to have Claire Fairchild as a friend.

Three

Saturday, May 6

I'd slept well that night, looking forward to the next time Claire and I would get to spend time together. I couldn't believe she'd stood up to my mother, and the memory of it made me grin as I brushed Rocinante's shiny brown coat.

The colt perked his ears and raised his head in the direction of the stable door. Out of the corner of my eye, I saw a shadow fall onto the hay-sprinkled ground, and I presumed it was Jesse, the stable boy. But I was delighted to have been mistaken.

"If I didn't know any better, I'd say you're up to some

kind of mischief," Claire said with a hint of a smirk. She wore a frock much like the one from the day before, only it was pale lavender with thick yellow threading. Her cheeks were extra rosy, like she'd run the whole way from her uncle's place, and her hair fell down her back in a soft straw-colored sheet.

I dropped the brush into the basket and put my hands on my hips. "What if I am?"

"Then I want in, of course."

I racked my brain trying to come up with something extraordinary to do. I'd hoped to pick the apple I'd discovered the day before, but I doubted Claire would consider that particular plan impressive, let alone "mischievous."

"That's a beautiful horse," Claire said, reaching out to pet Rocinante.

He sniffed her hand. I opened my mouth to warn her he wasn't good with strangers, something he'd proven over and over again since his mother had died. However, to my amazement, he not only allowed Claire to stroke his neck, but he stepped closer so she could better reach him, lowering his head so she could scratch his ears.

She laughed. "I think he likes me."

While she continued to pet him, I picked up where I'd left off brushing him. "This is Rocinante. He lost his mother when he was very young. I hand-fed him for quite a few weeks, and ever since, I've had a special spot for him in my heart."

"Well, I can certainly see why," she said. "He's very special."

"Thank you," I said. "Do you ride?"

"A little."

"Then it's settled." I stepped outside and called to the stable boy. "Jesse, will you prepare Opal and Rocinante? We are going riding." Then I smiled at my friend. "Let's go to my house so you can change clothes."

The sweet aroma of apple blossoms filled the air as we walked up the road. Claire reached up with her long, slender arm and touched a branch, which gave me an idea. What if Claire could help me pick the mysterious apple I'd discovered? She was certainly tall enough to give me the boost I needed.

"I have a favor to ask," I said, leading her off the road and into the orchard.

"All right. What is it?" she asked.

As we meandered through the trees, I took her a little ways off the path to keep her from noticing the trunk in which I'd carved R+J a few weeks before. Once we arrived at the center of the orchard, I pointed at the lone apple among the budding leaves and fragrant blossoms.

She stared at it, agape. "I don't know about here, but in Port Bennett, apples aren't ready until late summer, early autumn."

"I think that's the way it is everywhere. That's why I want to pick it."

"It's too high. You might get hurt," she said.

"Really, Claire." I crossed my arms over my chest. "You're beginning to sound like my mother. If you'll lift me up to that branch, I can climb the rest of the way."

She sighed. "Very well. Please be careful."

Using the trunk as support, I placed my boot in her

cupped hands and she hoisted me up. I missed the branch the first two times, but on our third attempt, I got a firm hold of it. It took some doing, but I was luckily able to pull myself up and climb even higher. Finally, I wrapped my hand around the bright red fruit and gave it a tug. "Got it!"

"Here, toss it down."

Once Claire caught it, I started making my way down. When I finally reached the lowest branch, I held on and swung my legs down, my feet dangling in midair. I gasped. On the way up, it hadn't seemed quite so high.

"I'll catch you. You can do it," Claire said, obviously sensing my fear. She set the apple down and held up her arms.

"It's all right," I said breathlessly. "I'll jump."

She backed up, giving me room.

I counted in my mind: *three, two, one.* Then I closed my eyes, held my breath, and dropped to the ground. My landing was far from graceful, yet I was glad I didn't twist an ankle or otherwise hurt myself.

Claire polished the fruit on the sleeve of her dress

before handing it over. I turned it in my hands. It was red as blood and completely symmetrical. Though I looked closely, I saw no wormholes, bruises, or even a speckle marring its smooth, gleaming skin. "It's the most perfect apple I've ever seen," I said.

Claire and I headed to the stairs, but Claire lingered in the dining hall to admire the enormous family portrait monopolizing the wall. "This painting is exquisite," she said, focusing on the signature at the bottom right corner. "I haven't heard of Jasper B. Holding, but surely he is a famous artist in these parts."

"Not yet," I said, swooning as I pictured Jasper's handsome face—with eyes the color of the sea and a mop of shiny reddish-brown hair—in my mind's eye. "He's only eighteen, and it seems the most famous ones are much older."

"If not dead," Claire said.

"True. I do think Jasper will make a name for himself someday, and well before he's dead. Anyway, he's the one who gives me painting lessons. He insists it is enough to keep him happy, but I know his dream is to have steady work painting portraits for the most affluent families in the land." I didn't like to think about Jasper working for someone else, even though it would be much better for his career. I guess I wasn't too keen on sharing him, and I definitely didn't wish to lose him.

"Are you blushing?" Claire asked, and under her scrutiny, my cheeks felt even warmer. She put her hands on her hips. "Regina, are you pining for your art teacher?"

"Don't be foolish. Of course not," I said, praying my mother hadn't heard her. "Now, come," I said, waving her along.

"He certainly has talent," Claire said, giving the portrait one last glance before falling into step with me.

Four

February, three months earlier

"Are you certain this is the artist Leopold uses?" hissed my mother through the side of her mouth.

Neither my father nor I answered. We stood as we'd been arranged, flanking the deep red chair in which my mother sat. Her back straight and her hands in her lap, she drummed her bejeweled fingers. I couldn't see her face from where I stood, but I had a hunch her eyes were glazed and she wore a hint of a smile—or, probably, more of a smirk. If the artist—Jasper, I think he'd said he was called—knew best, he'd make my mother appear even more beautiful in his painting than she actually was.

Then it was possible she'd forgive him for taking longer than she wanted.

Although I did not enjoy standing still for hours, either, I was not nearly as antsy as my mother for Jasper to finish. I liked the way he tilted his head when he studied each of us, and the way he chuckled softly to himself whenever Thaddeus, the faithful bloodhound sleeping peacefully yet noisily at my father's feet, grunted. Every now and then, Jasper squinted his eyes or wrinkled his forehead. Once or twice, he stepped away from the painting, studying it for a few minutes before picking up his paintbrush again.

I could tell when he was painting me. Whenever I dared to meet his gaze, it felt as if his eyes were probing into my very soul, viewing my secrets and dreams. At first it was overwhelming, and it gave me a funny feeling in the pit of my stomach. While I tried to focus on the window behind him—he'd wanted natural light to help bring out our features—some mysterious force kept pulling me back to his eyes. They were unlike any I'd ever seen: bluish green, framed by thick, dark lashes. They seemed to twinkle, and when he raised the corner of his mouth, giving me a crooked grin, it felt as though my heart skipped a beat. I wore a dress my mother had commissioned for the occasion, one that would appear fashionable and classic for all the years the painting—if my mother ended up favoring it—would bedeck our wall. Yet the way the artist's eyes roved over every part of me, I felt as if I were wearing a much more revealing garment—or perhaps nothing at all. Thinking those sorts of thoughts made my cheeks heat up. Hopefully, Jasper wouldn't capture my blush in his painting. Unless, of course, it made me look more beautiful.

Weeks later, Jasper delivered the finished portrait, and as my parents discussed where to hang it, I followed him to the door. "You paint very well," I said. "My mother is pleased, and that is no easy feat."

He flashed his crooked smile, rendering me speechless. The sudden silence between us made me nervous, and so I added, "I wish I could paint well."

"Who says you can't?" he asked.

"Well, no one has actually *said* I can't. It's just that I—"

"Haven't tried?"

I nodded.

"Well, that should be remedied."

I wasn't sure what he meant, but I liked the sound of it. As Solomon closed the door behind him, the idea struck me. "Jasper, wait," I called, running outside.

He glanced up from his cart and brushed his hair out of his eyes.

"Will you teach me?" I bit my lower lip, trying not to blush again. "I don't know if my parents will agree to it," I said, though I knew it was only my mother I'd need to convince, "but if so, will you teach me?"

"Work it out with your parents," he said, "and we will see. You strike me as a girl who gets what she wants. Maybe not straightaway, but eventually."

Back in the dining hall, I sat on the window ledge for quite some time, debating what the best way would be to present the notion of art lessons to my mother. She appeared to be genuinely happy with the portrait, barking directives at my father to make sure it was centered above the hearth. "I said two fingers' width to the left, Henry."

He obeyed, only to have her move it two fingers' width to the right.

"You look so beautiful, Mother," I remarked, observing the picture. "The artist really has a gift. Don't you agree?"

"Surprisingly, he did not disappoint," she said.

"He mentioned he could teach me. After my academic lessons, of course."

My father climbed down and adjusted his jacket. "I think it's a fine idea," he said, a little winded. "What do you say, Cora, my dear? Regina's artwork would make a wonderful addition to our library and study, don't you agree?"

"You wish to learn how to paint?" my mother asked. She eyed me suspiciously, and I knew that if I wanted her blessing, I could not let her suspect that more than learning how to paint, I wanted to learn about the young man who'd be teaching me.

"Very much so," I said with a nod.

My mother pressed her lips together. It took great self-control not to plead with her as she considered her answer. Inside, I was begging: *Please say yes!*

She sighed. "Very well, Regina. I will make the arrangements." After she turned on her high heels and walked out of the room, I beamed at my father.

For my first art lesson, a surprisingly temperate February afternoon, Jasper Holding met me out in the courtyard. He wore a white shirt that was a little too large on his slim frame, the top few buttons undone, and dark brown pants that were frayed at the hem, which was only noticeable up close. Fortunately, up close to Jasper was where I found myself, near enough to smell the paint on his hands.

"What is your passion, Regina?" he asked as he set up my paints and a modest piece of canvas, which was the size of my boot.

I lowered the hood of my cloak. "I'm not sure I know what you mean."

"What do you care most about?"

I scanned the horizon, as I often did, searching for my answer. And there he was: Rocinante, his dark brown coat glistening in a surprise appearance of February sunshine.

Jasper followed my gaze and nodded understandingly. "Paint a picture of your steed."

I did as he said, taking my time, listening to Jasper's instructions and adding my own touches whenever inspiration tickled my fancy. I had the curves of Rocinante's bones and the markings on his muzzle memorized, as well as the way his big brown eyes sparkled when I spotted my reflection in them. By the end of the session, I believed I'd done a commendable job. I was curious what Jasper thought of it, though.

"What do you think?" I asked.

Jasper studied it and then turned his bluish-green gaze on me. "It's rather good, especially considering it's your first painting and horses are never easy. I'm not so sure about the trees, though."

"I added those to make it look more realistic," I explained. "It's a whole scene, rather than just a horse in the middle of the canvas."

"Which trees are they?"

I pointed to the small patch of leafless elms that bordered the stables.

"Ah. That's what I suspected. Look closer, Regina. They don't have perfectly straight trunks and symmetrical branches."

I bit my lower lip, feeling foolish. Of course, he was right. The trees I'd painted looked ridiculous.

"May I?" he asked, gesturing at my seat.

I nodded, and after helping me up, he sat at the easel. Not ten minutes later, he'd added texture, bumps, and slight curves. Like magic, the trees he'd painted mirrored the actual ones.

"That's amazing," I said, truly impressed and suddenly eager to show my mother.

He shrugged modestly. "Keep in mind for next time that nothing found in nature is truly perfect."

Saturday, May 6

Once I showed Claire my room, she gasped and her jaw went slack. "Your bedroom is the size of my entire house." She spun around like she was performing a maypole dance.

I imagined what it would look like through Claire's eyes—the ornately carved four-poster bed; the dresser spilling over with jewelry boxes and figurines; the finest linens, drapes, wallpaper, and rug—and realized it must seem excessive. "My mother never seems to be satisfied with what we have; she always wants more," I tried to explain as I placed the apple on my bedside table.

Running her fingers through the golden tassels that adorned a pillow, she said, "Your mother has very fine taste in these sorts of things." Even though Claire had a point, I couldn't help grimacing at the compliment. It was one thing to try to win my mother's approval, but why put forth so much effort when she wasn't there to hear?

"She would certainly agree with you," I said. "I'm sure your mother has excellent taste, as well."

"Oh." Claire's shoulders shrunk, and she appeared to deflate before my very eyes. "I don't know about that. I guess she works with what we have."

"What is *your* family like?" I asked. Though I was eager to know her better, I mainly wanted to change the topic of conversation. It was bad enough that my mother haunted my every waking moment—and a good number of sleeping ones, too. I was hoping my new companion would grant me a much-desired reprieve.

"My family? Well, it's not nearly as interesting as yours, I'm afraid," she said, wandering around my room with her hands clasped behind her back. "Our most fascinating tale is about my mother's widowed younger brother. When Uncle Giles was fourteen, he discovered an old man's body washed up on the shore. He gave the man his own breath and was able to save his life. The old man happened to be King Leopold's royal doctor, and he was so grateful to my uncle, he made him his apprentice. When the old man died some years later, my uncle took over. Now he is the royal doctor, living in a mansion near the castle. But of course you already know that story."

"Actually, this is the first I've heard of his beginnings," I said. I'd never really wondered about Giles's past, as I assumed he'd always been affluent. He sure acted like it, anyway. Then again, so did my mother.

Flinging open the wardrobe doors, I said, "Give me a moment, and I'll find something for you to wear."

While I busied myself selecting riding attire for Claire, she was admiring the vial of rose water my mother had brought back for me from her trip to the eastern coast. Claire unscrewed the delicate top and sniffed its sweet fragrance.

"Have you a beau back home in Port Bennett?" I asked.

"Goodness, no. What would make you think that?"

"The ring you wear around your neck. I thought maybe it was a gift from someone special."

She set the rose water down and tucked the ring down the front of her dress. "No, I don't have a beau," she said, lowering her eyes.

I decided not to probe any further. As I carried the clothes over to her, she hopped on the bed and wallowed on the woven silk bedspread as if it were nothing better than stitched-together flour sacks. I gasped out loud. No one ever sat on the bedspreads, let alone rolled around on them. *My mother would have a conniption if she saw Claire doing that,* I thought.

At first I was aghast, but after the thought had a chance to simmer for a few seconds, I started giggling.

I tossed the clothes on the floor and jumped onto my bed. After we'd bludgeoned one another with the pillows, we flung the rest of the linens into the air, making a magnificent mess. Claire crossed her eyes and I squirted rose water down her back. I laughed harder and harder until an unladylike snort escaped.

A knock on the door brought us both to attention. We struggled to stop laughing. My eyes darted around the room, taking in the mess of blankets and pillows—along with, regrettably, the beads, tassels, and ribbons that had burst loose from their moorings. There wasn't time to clean up. Whoever waited on the other side of the door had caught us red-handed and pink-cheeked. If it was my mother, I feared she'd find Claire an unsuitable companion for me.

"Who is it?" I asked, trying to make my tone sound innocent.

"Forgive me for interrupting," Rainy said through the cracked door.

Relief pulsed through my veins. "You may come in," I said.

"Good day, m'lady. And good day to you, Miss Claire. When will you two be taking your midday meal?"

"Actually, Rainy, could you pack us a picnic?" I asked.

"Yes, m'lady. Where, might I ask, are you young ladies off to on this fine spring day?" She ambled around the room, tidying up.

"We have no idea," I replied, handing the riding clothes to Claire.

"It sounds like the perfect destination," Rainy said with a wink. She continued cleaning my room until she happened upon the apple. Claire and I must have knocked it off the table while we were horsing around.

"How curious," she said, examining the red fruit as Claire and I had previously done. "Where did you find an apple this time of year?"

"In the orchard," I said.

"We picked it only moments ago," Claire added as I showed her to the changing area. While she dressed, I picked up a pair of far-flung pillows.

Rainy smoothed the tatted doily on my bedside table before setting the apple on it. "You'd best eat it before your father catches sight of it," she said, wagging her finger.

"I'm going to give it to my art teacher when he comes on Tuesday."

Rainy chuckled. "An apple for the teacher. How quaint!"

After she left to prepare our picnic, Claire emerged from behind the screen. "How do I look?" she asked. My riding pants were admittedly too baggy and short for her. However, Claire didn't seem to mind. As for the teal jacket, it fit perfectly, as if it had been tailored especially for her.

If we had this much fun getting ready to go riding, I could only imagine how wonderful the ride itself would be.

Five

I gave Rocinante a swift kick with my heels, and he obediently hastened into a canter. The pine trees whisked by as his hooves skimmed along the sweet-smelling field of fresh spring grass and wildflowers. I was truly my happiest when I was riding with the graceful, powerful movement of the horse beneath me and the wind in my face. The wonderful sense of freedom that came with it was what I imagined it would feel like to fly.

On Rocinante's back, I could escape my reality for a while. I could get away from my mother's demands, from having to be poised and polite to people who didn't know the real me. People I didn't care to know at all. Of course, when we got back to the stable, my problems would be waiting for me again. Even so, they somehow seemed more bearable after a good long ride.

"Oh my goodness! Whoa, Opal! Whoooooooah!" Claire shouted.

I'd almost forgotten I had company. I reined to the side, and still running, Rocinante moved over so I could catch sight of Claire. As Opal trotted, Claire bumped up and down, making a terrible smacking sound each time she hit the saddle—which was never in the same place twice. If her face hadn't been contorted in pain and fear, I would have found the scene quite amusing.

I urged Rocinante alongside Opal and leaned over to catch the mare's rein in my hand. "Easy, Opal." With a gentle tug, I slowed her until both horses were walking. "Good, good," I said once she eased into a gentle, steady pace.

Beads of perspiration dotted Claire's forehead, and her lower lip trembled. "Thank you, Regina. Oh, my. That was . . . exhilarating."

We rode side by side through the meadow and she fell in line behind me as we switchbacked up a tree-covered hill. Once on top, we could see a great deal of the Enchanted Forest, which appeared even more enchanting than usual, as it was bathed in golden sunlight.

"I feel like I'm on top of the world," Claire said, sounding winded.

"That's why I like coming here." I gave Rocinante a good rub on his neck, and his tail swished merrily.

A pair of twittering bluebirds danced in the sky above our heads and glided off, down the north face of the hill. "Oh! That must be Leopold's castle," Claire said, pointing in the direction in which the birds had disappeared.

Despite the distance at which it stood, the castle's magnificence was palpable. Its stony turrets rose high above the tallest trees, piercing the underbellies of the clouds. "It is," I said, dismounting and helping Claire do the same. We led the horses to a bubbling stream, where I took their reins and all four of us quenched our thirst.

"Have *you* ever been inside?" Claire asked as she

collected some water in her cupped hands. "Have you ever met King Leopold or Queen Eva?" She took a quick sip and blotted her mouth dry with the edge of her—or rather, *my*—riding jacket.

"Not yet," I answered for both of her questions. I felt my jaw muscles tense.

Claire stopped drinking and fixed her eyes on me. "What is it, Regina? You can trust me. I am your friend."

In my entire sixteen years, no one had ever said those words to me. The moment felt surreal. Even stranger, I actually sensed I *could* trust Claire. "I'm afraid of what will happen when my mother sees the king and queen after all this time," I confessed. "They may be the rulers of the land, but my mother, well, she . . ."

"Is a powerful sorceress," Claire supplied for me.

I laughed. "Yes, you could say that."

"By the sound of it, your mother already got her revenge on Eva for having tripped her. Your mother spun straw into gold, Regina. And she married your father, the prince. It's not every day a miller's daughter becomes a royal."

"True," I agreed. "However, my mother believes the score is unsettled. After all, she is married to a prince, but—"

"Eva's husband is a king," Claire finished for me, and I nodded.

Deep down, I knew it wasn't a question of *if* but *when* my mother would exact a terrible revenge on the queen. I just hoped it wouldn't have the upcoming ball—and my father, Claire, and me—as a backdrop.

"Well, then." I was more than ready to switch up our conversation, preferably to one having nothing to do with marrying a king, as I got more than my fair share of that particular topic from my mother. "Are you ready to continue? Just a little farther, and you'll get to see the royal gardens," I said over my shoulder as I began gathering the horses. "There's a giant maze made entirely of hedges, a lovely little brook, and the most charming bridge you've ever seen, with pink rosebushes on either end of it. Beyond the bridge, there's an elegant fountain straight out of a storybook." The first time I'd been there, I was about six. My father had taken me on the back of

Hwin, Rocinante's late mother. It had felt like a dream, and I'd wanted to become one of the many butterflies or birds that lived in the gardens so I could stay there forever.

"It sounds like the perfect place for a picnic," Claire said.

We mounted our horses and had traveled for about twenty minutes when we spotted a woman ahead of us on the road. She had a disastrous nest of blond hair and wore a flowing black dress unlike any I'd ever seen, with a neckline that came to points like the sepal of a rose. She clutched her knapsack with haggard hands and jerked her chin skyward. I had to keep a gasp from slipping out, because when she twisted to look at us, her eyes were a shocking milky blue.

Claire gave me a wee frown when she, too, realized the woman was blind. "Have you lost your way, perchance?" Claire asked.

The woman hunched her shoulders and hugged her bag protectively against her rounded bosom. "What is it to you?" she snapped.

"We mean you no harm," I said, hoping to calm her down. "We will be on our way."

Claire shrugged and we nudged our horses into motion.

"Wait," the woman called a second or two after we'd passed. Claire and I exchanged a look and pulled our reins. "I'm not lost." She laughed breathily and kicked up one of her pointy-toed boots. "Rather, I've wandered farther than I should have, and now my legs are weary." Her voice had sweetened considerably, and she sounded almost as if she were singing. "Please, will you give me a ride? I live over yonder," she said, flapping one of her hands to the west.

"Of course we will." As Claire spoke, her fingers grazed the ring she wore on her necklace. "Won't we, Regina?"

I hesitated. "What about the royal gardens?" I whispered to Claire.

"I can see them another day," she said.

"Oh, you have things to do," the woman said in a singsong. "Do not worry about me, no, no, no. I will make my way home before the wolves come out. Do not worry about the poor blind lady."

I sighed. "Very well. You can ride on the back of my horse."

The woman wiggled her fingertips and gave a little hop-skip as I turned Rocinante around and helped her get on—a simpler task than I'd expected, given her blindness and her refusal to let go of her knapsack.

"Go thataway, and soon the road will give way to a footpath," she said, holding out her left arm. As we rode deeper and deeper into the woods, she hummed to herself.

We wove through the towering trees with moss-covered trunks, the horses' hooves cushioned by leaves and pine needles. We passed through sunny patches of grass and flowers, as well as shady spots of toadstools and leafy canopy. We pushed through some particularly large ferns and finally caught our first glimpse of the woman's home.

At first I thought my near-empty stomach was

playing a cruel trick on me, but even after I blinked, the cottage still appeared to be made of gingerbread, cake, frosting, and candies. Not only was it built entirely of treats, but it smelled like them, too; the delicious aroma of freshly baked cake filled my nose. Even as my mouth began watering and the urge to feast on sweets overcame me, I heard my mother's warning in the back of my mind: *If you're to become queen, you'd best stay away from baked goods.*

"A cottage made of confections . . ." Claire said, her eyes wide. "I've never seen such a thing."

The woman tittered as she slid off Rocinante's back. "I should hope not," she said. "This is my creation, and it's one of a kind. Always has been, always will be." She stood on the pathway that led to the front door and sniffed the air. "I baked a cake earlier this morn. Come in and have a piece, won't you? It's the least I can do to repay you for your kindness."

"We really mustn't," I said. "I need to be back for afternoon tea. But thank you all the same."

"Oh, but Regina! It smells *delicious*," Claire said. She

had already dismounted and was tying Opal to a nearby tree, as surely any horse would chew through the licorice and peppermint-stick fence. "We won't stay long. Besides, it'll do my body some good to take a break before riding back home," she added, rubbing her rear end and pulling a face so funny I couldn't help laughing out loud.

"Good girl," the lady said. "Now, come inside. Don't tarry."

I watched Claire follow the woman inside, and from what I could see through the door she'd left ajar for me, the interior was made of sweets, too. I took a few steps forward and then stopped. I suddenly had a bad feeling.

Is there magic here? And if so, is it light or dark?

Yet I couldn't very well let Claire go in alone.

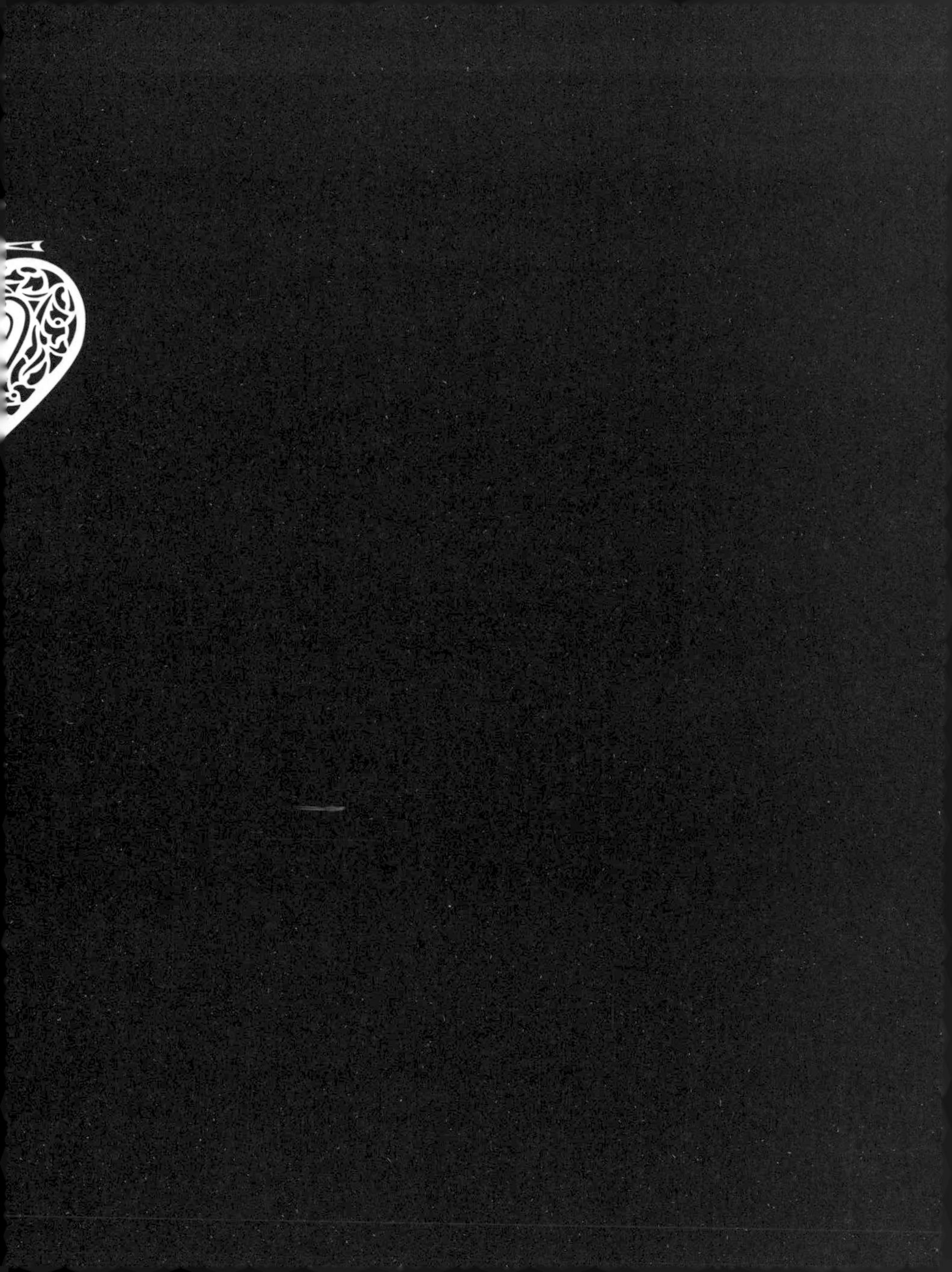

Six

The gingerbread walls were adorned with icing and peppermint candies in pretty designs of flowers, dots, and squiggles. On a table in the center of the room, a sugar-crystal candelabrum was surrounded by a smorgasbord of pastries. The aroma of freshly baked cake was almost dizzying once I was inside.

"Don't mind the dust. I need to find someone to give this place a good spring cleaning," the woman said when I stepped into the quaint living room. "I've put the kettle on, so we can have hot cocoa." She rubbed her hands together and hummed an odd little tune.

I breathed a little easier when I saw Claire sitting in a cushiony chair, looking completely at ease as she sampled the piece of strawberry cake the woman had given her. Maybe my qualms were unfounded after all.

Claire pointed at the dessert with her fork. "This is the best cake I've had in my entire life." She took another couple of bites and said with her mouth full, "Come on, Regina. Have some."

"Try one of these meringue delights," the woman said to me, holding out a dainty yellow cookie that spiraled up into a perfect peak. I placed it in my mouth, and the flavor of sugar and lemon exploded on my tongue. "Yes, yes, and here's one for you." She gave a cookie to Claire.

"I've never seen so many goodies," Claire said. "Tell me, are you a baker? A candymaker? Do you work for the king? Because if not, you definitely should."

The woman tittered as she lowered her body into the chair next to Claire's. "Goodness, no, no, no. I am what I am, nothing more, nothing less."

While Claire ate the rest of her cake and kept the woman engaged in conversation, I took a look around. Other than the array of sweets, the cottage was sparsely decorated. I glanced down the corridor and spied the strap of the woman's knapsack poking out from behind a narrow green door. Curious as to what she'd been packing all that time, I tiptoed down the hallway.

I bit back a gasp as I peered into the room. It was packed with baskets and trunks, each bursting with diamonds and other jewels, gold, and silver. At my feet, a handful of rubies spilled out of the knapsack she'd been carrying. *How has she acquired all this wealth?* I wondered. Even if she supplied the castle with her confectionary masterpieces every single day, I couldn't imagine King Leopold would pay her *that* much. Had she inherited it, by chance? Could she, like my mother, use magic to turn something as mundane as straw into riches? Or had she stolen all of it?

The woman seemed harmless enough, but perhaps she befriended strangers in the woods only to turn around and rob them. Ogres were known to feign being hurt or trapped, luring unsuspecting humans into elaborate schemes that ended tragically for the humans.

I couldn't let the blind woman know I'd discovered her trove. All the horrible possibilities ran amok in my mind and made the hairs on the back of my neck bristle. I took one last glance at the treasure—partly to make sure it was real, and partly because it was such a strange and beautiful sight—and then hurried back to the living room, just as the kettle whistled from the kitchen.

"Would you like me to make the hot cocoa?" Claire asked the woman.

I shook my head at Claire, hoping to make her understand we needed to leave. However, she whisked by me, just out of my reach, saying, "Don't worry, Regina. I'll be quick about it."

"I'll help," I said, desperate to get Claire alone so I could warn her.

"No, no, no," the woman said, springing to her feet and rushing into the kitchen. "I must do it, only me. Sit, be my guest."

"All right," Claire said, shrugging, as she returned to the living room.

As I followed Claire, the woman materialized in front of me. Somehow, she'd made the cocoa, poured it into three mugs, and arranged them on a doily-covered tray, all in mere seconds. She swayed from side to side, and not a drop of hot cocoa spilled; in fact, it didn't even slosh. "Stay out of my kitchen!"

I backed off, shocked at what I was witnessing. "How did you do that?"

"Never mind what you think you heard, never mind what you think you saw, never mind what you think you know," she blathered. "It's time for hot cocoa, and that is *that*." Her blind eyes bored into me, and her unruly blond hair thrashed about as if it were alive.

"Regina, what are you doing?" Claire asked from behind me.

"We're saying good-bye. We're leaving," I said, reaching for my friend's hand. But the woman held out the tray at arm's length and Claire took it, instead. Out of the corner of my eye, I thought I saw the cupcakes and pies and other treats in the dining room floating up into the air. But in a blink, the pastries were on the table, as before.

"Come, sit, sip the sweet chocolate," the woman sang as she shooed us away from the kitchen and back into the little living room.

"Trust me, Claire. We have to go," I whispered into my friend's ear as the woman continued her ditty. "Something's not right. She's a witch of some sort, I swear to you."

"If what you say is true," Claire whispered back, "we mustn't anger her."

Claire carried the tray over to the coffee table and set it down. Once the woman sat in her chair, Claire placed a cup of cocoa in her hands, and then she slowly, quietly poured the two meant for us into the fireplace. "Mmmm," she said as she handed me an empty mug.

Grinning, the woman took a sip for herself. "Oh my stars!" She leapt to her feet. "I forgot the sweet cream. Sit, wait, I'll be right back with it."

"You needn't bother," Claire said. "It's quite delicious without the cream. The best I've ever had, truth be told."

"Actually . . ." I countered, seeing an opportunity to sneak out—although, based on the time it took her to make the cocoa in the first place, we'd have to run as fast as we could. "I'd like some cream. Some more cocoa, too, if it's no bother."

"Oh, goody. We've a smart cookie amongst us." She whirled around, her cloudy eyes moving about the room. "I must start again. Give me the mugs." She held out her hands, which were flinching, like they were being stung by bees.

"Yes, yes, of course." I began placing the mugs on the tray, two empty and one full.

The woman lingered by the mantel, her nose twitching and nostrils flaring. All of a sudden, she bent down and sniffed the chocolate-drenched log.

Claire and I exchanged wide-eyed glances, knowing the witch was onto us. With my head, I gestured for Claire to make a run for the door, but she only took a few steps. Meanwhile, the witch stood and turned to face me. It was as if she'd grown to twice her previous height. I held out the tray, ready to run. "Here you go."

The witch raised her gnarled hands high in the air, knocking the tray to the floor. The broken mugs made a terrible crunching sound as she stepped on them with her pointy-toed boots. "Liars!" she screamed, pointing all ten of her fingers at us.

"My ring!" Claire cried. Sure enough, the witch was wearing Claire's ring on her thumb.

With a tornado-like force, Claire and I were lifted off our feet. We flew head over heels out the front door, landing in heaps on the hard ground outside.

When I swiped my hair out of my eyes and glanced up to see if Claire was all right, I saw that her jacket—my jacket, rather—was splattered with hot cocoa. Otherwise, I was relieved to see we were alive and as well as could be expected. Although Rocinante and Opal neighed and pawed the dirt, they seemed to be all right, too.

Claire scrambled to her feet and began dusting off. "That horrid woman took my ring."

"Wait. Where are you going?" I asked as she stormed toward the cottage.

"To get it back," she said.

The door slammed shut before us, and the drapes dropped over the sugar-coated windowpanes.

"Claire, stop. Please." I wanted to help her, but I couldn't form the words. Plain and simple, I was too scared. "That woman, she has magic. It's too dangerous."

When Claire turned to look at me, I thought I glimpsed a tear in her eye. However, her lips were pressed together in determination. "I want it back," she said softly. "That nasty witch."

"I know. We will figure something out. I promise. But for now, we must get out of here."

When I handed Opal's reins to Claire, my arm felt tender, and I predicted an ugly black-and-blue bruise was on its way. Before mounting Rocinante, I glanced back at the cottage. It might have been the way the shadows dappled it, but it appeared much of the gingerbread had cracked and chipped off, and in place of the sweet aromas we'd originally been treated to was the unsavory stench of something burning. Somehow, I could still smell it even as we rode up to Giles's estate and I helped Claire get down from Opal.

"You were so quiet on the ride home, Claire. What are you thinking about?" I asked as I attached the lead to Rocinante's halter.

"I know it sounds silly, but I wanted to give my brother's ring to my firstborn . . . if I'm fortunate enough to become a mother, that is. In that small way, my child would be able to know how brave his or her uncle was, and how he'd sacrificed his life for Ma and me. I want my child to know that Corbin Fairchild was a hero." She made a small hiccup sound and covered her mouth for a second.

"Oh, Claire. That doesn't sound silly at all."

"Thank you. But you are right, Regina."

"Right? About what?"

"The danger. The witch has magic. Besides, she'll probably peddle my brother's ring long before we can go back for it."

"I don't think the witch's magic is very strong," I said.

"Not anywhere as powerful as my mother's, for instance."

"Do you think your mother would retrieve my ring for me?" Claire asked.

"Oh. I don't know." I swallowed, hoping to get rid of the lump in my throat. "She wouldn't be happy about my having gone to the witch's cottage in the first place. . . ." I didn't even want to imagine what kind of punishment she'd dole out if she discovered I'd put myself in harm's way by keeping company with a bad witch.

Claire touched my elbow. "It's all right. I understand. And really, who can blame her for wanting to keep her only child safe and sound?"

In the quiet moment that followed, a bluebird landed on a branch above us, and soon after, another swooped in and nuzzled against it.

"Claire, may I ask you something personal?"

"Of course." She turned, focusing her bright eyes on me. "I'm your friend. I have no secrets from you." Claire held out her arms and not a second later, we were hugging. I squeezed her, feeling her warmth wash over me.

"I'll always keep your secrets as if they were my own," she said gravely as we let go.

If ever there were magic words, Claire had just uttered them. I felt a sense of freedom so light and pure, I wanted nothing more than to pour out my soul to my dear confidante. "Do you ever wish you had magic, Claire?" I asked. "Just a little? Enough to protect yourself, as well as anyone else who doesn't have it?"

"Like back there at the gingerbread cottage?" she asked, and I nodded.

"Also, so I wouldn't be so afraid of my mother," I confessed.

Claire inclined her head and squinted, as if contemplating her response. I realized I might have offended her in some way, or perhaps I'd put her in a tough position, as my mother had been kind enough to bring her here from the far side of the Enchanted Forest. "You want to learn magic to use against your mother?" she asked, finally.

When she put it that way, it made me sound evil,

and I didn't want Claire to think of me that way. "Only a touch of magic," I said, holding my thumb and forefinger a small space apart. "Mainly, so my mother doesn't always have the upper hand. I hate always fearing what she's going to do next. It may be something small, like changing my clothes if she disapproves of my choice, or locking me in my room when she's had enough of me. Sometimes it's much worse. Much . . . darker." I chose not to think about all the abhorrent things I suspected my mother had had her hand in: the memories I'd attempted to block or explain away as happenstance. It was too upsetting—especially since I was helpless to do anything about it. "When I was younger, I remember wishing my mother didn't have magic, or would somehow lose it. Now that I am older, I wonder if instead of wishing her to be without magic, maybe the answer is for me to learn it. After all, wouldn't it make sense, since it's in my blood, too?"

"Claire, say good-bye to Regina. It's time to come in," Giles called from the balcony, and his boisterous voice gave me a jolt.

"Yes, Uncle," she responded to him. Then, holding my shoulder, she asked quietly, "How do you intend to learn magic, Regina?"

I bit my lower lip for a second. "Like my mother did, I suppose. I will have to find someone to teach me."

We hugged good-bye, and then I began riding home, leading Opal behind me. It surprised me I trusted Claire enough to have shared my innermost thoughts with her. They'd been confined to my mind, yet they'd come out so willingly and freely in her company. She'd listened raptly, and even had a mist in her eyes. She understood. She truly was my friend, and I could tell her anything.

Seven

July, four years earlier

"My mother used to do my hair like this whenever I'd go riding," Rainy said as she licked her fingers and wetted down the small hairs of my part. Next she passed me a handheld mirror and twisted my chair so I could see the back of my head in the larger mirror hanging on my bedroom wall. "Take a look-see, m'lady. What do you think?"

She'd styled my hair into two braids, looped them, and fastened them with long yellow ribbons at the nape of my neck. "I love it!" I said. And this time, I was being honest, rather than saying so to spare her feelings. "Where did you get the ribbons?"

"My daughter got them from the good doctor's wife when she was born," she said. "She won't mind your wearing them, not one bit."

"Thank you."

Rainy's dimples deepened and she curtsied. "I'm glad you're pleased."

A moment later, my mother bustled into the room with an armful of new gowns that she pushed into Rainy's hands. "There you are, Regina," she said, seemingly unaware—or more likely, unconcerned—that she'd nearly knocked the poor servant woman over. "I thought you were in the stable with that foal again." She pointed at my wardrobe, and I hurried to unlatch it so Rainy could hang the cumbersome dresses inside.

"I was, but then Father said he'd take me riding, so I came back here to change my clothes. He said since Rocinante is big enough to tag along with us, Hwin can finally get back out. Isn't that wonderful?" I'd begged to take Hwin out almost every day since her foaling, but my father kept telling me to be patient, that she wouldn't be too keen about leaving her baby behind. Two months was a long while to wait to ride my favorite horse.

"As long as you ride sidesaddle," my mother said, admiring herself in my mirror. "You must always ride like a lady." In the reflection, her gaze met mine. "Oh, Regina, *what* is going on with your hair?" she asked, scrunching her nose.

"I like it," I said softly. Out of the corner of my eye, I saw Rainy shrink behind the wardrobe.

My mother frowned as she reached for my head. "Well. You're twelve, not four." Two yellow ribbons fluttered down, landing on the rug. The braids fell down my back, unraveling. She gestured for me to sit in the chair, and I did. Soon after, she'd fixed my hair into a single braid, long and straight. "There, much better," she said, rubbing her hands together.

As soon as she left my bedroom, I crouched to scoop up the yellow ribbons. I tied them into a double bow at the tail end of my braid. Though Rainy said nothing, she nodded at me before following my mother out.

Jesse, our stable boy, jumped out of my way as I came barreling into the barn about twenty minutes later. "She's saddled and ready, my lady. Just don't go far. Rocinante's got himself some spindly little legs, and he might wear out quickly." He handed my cane to me. Jesse, my father, and I had an understanding. Whenever my mother was around, I was to ride sidesaddle. When she wasn't, they'd turn a blind eye so I could ride astride, or even bareback on special occasions.

My father was outside, tightening the girth around the mare's slimmed-down belly. "You should have seen how easily she took the bit," he said. "I'll say she's more than ready for a ride."

He boosted me up, and while I waited for him to mount his steed, I leaned forward to run my fingers through a small tangle in Hwin's mane. Not long ago, I would weave white flowers into her mane and parade her around the meadow. Even without the flowers, she looked like a princess's horse. Her bay coat gleamed a glossy dark brown, and Jesse had painted her hooves with polish so they matched her black mane.

I sat quietly in the saddle as the mare danced in place, doing a jig. Her ears swiveled around, flicking to and fro as she craned her neck, looking behind her for her baby.

"Don't worry, Hwin," I said, stroking the mare's silky neck. Her muscles rippled under her skin and she twitched, anxious about her first ride with her colt in tow. "He's coming, too."

The colt was stunning, just like his mother. Rocinante was a dark bay, and he had inherited his mother's blaze. He had a stubby tail that wasn't long enough yet to keep flies off, so he moved next to Hwin, who swished her tail over both their bodies. He cocked his sweet head and watched our every move with his liquid brown eyes.

"It won't be long till we get to go on longer rides, but for today, we will take it easy," I said, thinking he'd surely enjoy coming along with us to explore the world a little. My father and I squeezed our legs against our horses' sides and they moved into smooth walks, little Rocinante keeping up with his mother the entire length of the fence.

"We'll be back soon," my father called to Jesse as we marched the horses through the flat, open field.

Every so often, Hwin tugged on the bit. The reins slid through my fingers as I sat astride her. She blew out a breath, snorting and bobbing her head. She wanted to gallop, that much was clear, but she knew Rocinante wouldn't be able to keep up.

"You can go ahead if you'd like, Daddy." His horse was young and fast, and I was more than happy to stay back with the other two while his steed ran.

"You're sure you'll be all right?" he asked.

I smiled. "Of course. Now, go!"

He made a clicking sound with his tongue and loosened the reins. He gave his horse a kick and they took off for the rolling hills that bordered our estate. Rocinante began trotting, and his mother picked up the pace. I chuckled out loud at the look of determination in his eyes. We circled back around and entered a small patch of pines.

Suddenly, Hwin let out a panicked whinny. I wasn't sure what exactly had happened—maybe she'd lost sight of her baby for a moment—but she abruptly turned, and before I could react, I felt the sensation of my body flying through the air and coming into contact with something hard. It knocked the wind out of me and I struggled for breath as I lay on the ground. "It's all right," I said to the horses, fighting my instinct to cry as pain seared through my body. "I'm all right." Hwin stayed close by me, even when Rocinante decided to chase a pair of butterflies beyond the patch of trees.

I reached up to wipe the dirt and pine needles off my face, and I was shocked to see blood on my hands. *Oh, no, no, no. . . .* I tried to keep my eyes open, and I attempted to sit up, but the world was spinning. Just as everything went dark, I heard the sound of hoofbeats and my father calling, "Regina!"

"What is it? What happened to my daughter?" I heard my mother's voice, but it sounded muffled, as if I were underwater. I recalled hearing my father say something about my having fainted, and another man's voice assuring him it wasn't unusual for people to faint at the sight of their own blood.

I peeled open my eyes, trying to get them to focus. I was in my room, in my bed. The light was low and candles were lit, so I figured it must be dusk or even later. My mother shoved my father out of the way. I blinked two or three times as she leaned over my bed and placed her clammy palm on my throbbing forehead.

"I *said,* what happened?" she demanded.

Giles, our family doctor, stood at the opposite side of the bed from her and adjusted his spectacles. "There was an accident," he started.

"Well, of *course* it was an accident," she said with a subtle snort. "Regina would never harm herself on purpose."

He slid his glasses up his nose again. "Yes, right. I'm afraid young Regina got thrown by a horse."

"Thrown by a horse?" my mother repeated, turning from the doctor to her husband. "How could this have happened, Henry? I thought you've been working with her on her horsemanship. All those hours, all

the dust-covered pants and mud-splattered boots. And where were *you* while our daughter was off . . . getting *thrown?*"

From where I lay, I could see the sweat beading on my poor father's brow. Behind my mother's back, I caught his eye and shook my head ever so slightly. He swallowed hard. "I was with her, Cora. It happened so fast." He held out his hands, palms up, and added, "There's nothing I could have done to prevent it. You know if I could have, I would have. It pains me to see our darling daughter hurting."

"I see," my mother said in that horrible way that meant she didn't understand at all, and someone was going to pay.

"It's all right, dear. She's going to be fine," my father said. He reached out to touch her arm, but she shrugged away and leaned over me again.

"It's true, Cora," said Giles. "A few scrapes and bruises is all. This cut here," he said, pointing just above my lip, "is the deepest one. I've treated it with a potent salve, but chances are, it will leave a scar."

"A scar?" my mother asked, leaning in even closer. Her upper lip curled as she examined my face.

Giles nodded. "A small one. Barely even noticeable. There's plenty of salve here, so she can apply it morning and night."

"Thank you, Giles. Is your work here done?" she asked.

He cleared his throat. "I suppose it is."

"Very good. Rainy will see you out."

Not long after the doctor left, my mother smoothed back my hair and opened her palms. "No daughter of mine will have a scar marring her beautiful face," she said through clenched teeth. A purple cloud formed in her hands, and my father stepped back until he was flush against the wall.

In my woozy state, I mumbled, "What is it, Mother? Do you think no king will take me as his queen if I have a scar?"

The purple cloud grew and rose into the air. Once it started floating across the foot of my bed, I closed my eyes tightly. As a tingling sensation skimmed over my skin, I heard her voice, but it sounded like it was far away: "Oh, Regina. That's not it at all. Whenever you looked in the mirror and saw your scar, you'd remember the horrible experience of falling off a horse. You'd recall how it felt to not be in control of your own destiny. I did it for you, Regina. Don't you know by now? Everything I've done, and everything I do, is for you."

As soon as the tingles passed, I opened my eyes and saw her calm face. "Henry, bring us a mirror," she ordered. "There's one in the drawer in her vanity."

My father did as he was told. I gazed at my reflection in the looking glass. Thanks to magic, it appeared I hadn't had an accident at all. My face was as flawless as ever before.

"See, Regina? You're still the fairest of them all," my mother assured me.

Before she left me for the night, I said, "Hwin was only protecting her foal. She didn't mean to hurt me. She's a wonderful horse, and a good mother."

"I'm sure she is," my mother said, and with that, she blew out my candles.

All night long, I had nightmares, forcing me to relive the horror of falling off Hwin. In the wee hours of the morning, I awoke in a tangle of damp bed linens, and, staring at the underside of my canopy, forced myself to stay awake. I couldn't imagine getting up on Hwin's back again, and yet, I knew if I didn't, I would have to live in fear for the rest of my years.

A strange grunting noise came from beyond my open bedroom door. I swung my legs over the side of the bed and made out the shape of my father's beloved bloodhound sitting on his haunches in the hallway. "Why aren't you sleeping, Thaddeus? It's too early for breakfast." He grunted again, and I wondered if he was asking me the same question.

"I'm going for a ride." Saying the words aloud, even

if only to a dog, made my heart race and my hands sweat. "Don't tell anyone." He tilted his big brown-and-white head and then ambled back in the direction of my parents' chambers.

I padded over to my wardrobe and got dressed. The rooster hadn't yet crowed, and the sun hadn't yet climbed above the horizon. I thought if I waited, I might lose my courage. If that happened, I would never be able to get back up on the horse.

Once I entered the stable, little Rocinante trotted over to greet me, and I happily rewarded his friendliness with a handful of oats. I lightly stroked his muzzle as Hwin eagerly joined in. "I'm going to take your mama on a ride," I said to the foal. Hwin held her head up high and twitched her ears. "Are you surprised, sweet mama?" I laughed, but I admit it sounded like a nervous titter even to my own ears. "I guess I'm a little surprised, as well. Come, let's get you ready."

I'd watched Jesse prepare the horses enough times to know exactly how to do it, and in no time, Hwin was tacked up. "Let's do this, my friend," I said as I mounted her and sat astride her back. We took off in a walk, and slowly and smoothly progressed into a canter. She obeyed my every command with impressive precision, and though my heart beat hard, I finally started to relax into her. It was as if we weren't two, but one. Everything about it—from the early morning wind in my hair, to the feeling of being in this together with her, and, perhaps most importantly of all, the triumphant, powerful feeling that came from having conquered my fear—made me feel like I was flying.

The sun rose, washing the sky in orange and pink, and begrudgingly, I knew I'd best get home before my parents or a servant noticed my absence. As I slid from the saddle only moments later, I said, "We will ride again soon, Hwin."

Later that day, after I'd finished the last of my school lessons, I returned to the stables. Little Rocinante was whinnying—a high-pitched, scream-like sound, as if he was in agony. "Jesse, what's wrong with him?" I asked.

"Why is he scared? Put him in the stall with his mother, maybe that will help."

The stable boy stopped sweeping and looked up at me. His face was unusually pale. "Regina, I really don't think you should be here right now." He glanced at Hwin's stall and grimaced. "Please, go back to the house and don't come back until later this evening."

"Is something wrong with Hwin?" I peered over the stall door and my breath hitched. Hwin was flat on her side, unmoving. "Is she . . . ?" I couldn't bear to finish my question.

Jesse leaned on the broomstick and nodded miserably. "I don't know what happened. She seemed perfectly healthy last night."

And perfectly healthy early this morning, I added in my reeling mind. Yet there she was, dead.

I couldn't believe it. I didn't want to believe it.

All I could think to do was run. I fled across the meadow and up a tree-covered hill until I had to stop, unable to breathe for the heaviness of my heart.

Unwittingly, I'd returned to the very place of the accident. The soil, grasses, and wildflowers were smashed and upturned, and I spied dark brown splatters of my dried blood here and there. One of the yellow ribbons that had been in my hair dangled from the underside of a bush. I pulled it out, but it was frayed and dirty, and I was sure Rainy wouldn't want her daughter to have it back in such condition. I wasn't sure how long I sat against a tree, its pine needles pricking into the backs of my head and spine, before my father finally came for me.

"Daddy," I choked out between a fresh batch of sobs. He knelt beside me, and I placed the ribbon at his feet. Although he knew nothing about the ribbon, he shook his head sympathetically and rubbed my sore back. "Oh, Regina, I'm so sorry. I thought you'd be in the stables, so I went looking for you there. I saw what happened to poor Hwin. What a tragedy! We'll get through this together. You have to believe me. Chin up, my child." With that, he lifted my chin, and at that moment, I spotted the second ribbon. A robin must have swiped it, as it was woven into a nest high above our heads.

"Come, it's time for the evening meal," my father said, helping me to my feet. "The cooks have prepared something special for you." After we both dusted off our clothes, I placed my hand in his and gave the site of the accident one last glance. I was about to go back for the ribbon, but before I could, the robin swooped down and scooped it up in her dainty black beak. *It's just as well*, I thought as we made our way home.

"Why are you two late?" Mother demanded as soon as we washed up and entered the dining hall.

"The most horrible thing happened, Mother." I dabbed my tears with the linen napkin before spreading it in my lap. "Hwin. She's . . . she's . . ."

"She is no longer with us," my father finished for me.

I threw myself into my mother's arms, and I felt her take a sharp breath. "I'm sorry to hear that, my dear. I know you loved that horse." She gave my back a couple of pats and then held me at arm's length. "At least this way, she won't cause you harm, ever again."

I sat in my place at the dining table with my hands in my lap, as my belly was too upset to eat. I noticed my father's appetite wasn't the same, either, and he only ate about half of his turkey.

On the contrary, my mother seemed to relish her meal, and it made me question if she truly cared Hwin was dead. She finished every last ladylike bite, and after dabbing her lips with the fine linen napkin, she said, "How nice it must be to have such good food on the table every day. When I was your age, we often had nothing but beans." With her right eyebrow arched, she looked at me from across the table.

I did not know what she wanted me to say, so I tried the only thing I could think of. "I'm sorry, Mother."

Eight

Monday, May 8

It had been two days since I'd seen Claire, and I was beginning to miss her. As the hours trudged along, I began to worry. Had I scared her off with my talk about magic? Had she decided not to come around anymore? I wasn't quite sure how the rules of friendship worked.

One thing was going my way, though. My parents suspected nothing of our run-in with the blind witch. I'd been mindful of keeping my bruised arm hidden from view until it healed, which it had almost entirely, thanks to the salve Giles had given me years ago after I'd fallen off Hwin.

Not long after my parents and I had taken our morning meal, I retired to the living room to read a book while Thaddeus snored at my side. He suddenly lifted his head, a stream of drool dripping from his mouth. A second later, I heard it, too: the sound of horses pulling a carriage up our drive. The bloodhound promptly went back to his business of napping while I scrambled to my feet and dashed to open the front door, beating Solomon.

Giles's white carriage and two gray horses lurched to a stop. The carriage door swung open and Claire stepped out and down. She wore a rosebud-patterned shawl around her shoulders and a smile on her face. Once we greeted each other, she placed a small, flat parcel in my hands.

"What is this?" I asked.

"I washed and mended your riding jacket. It's not good as new, but I did my best." After I gave her a hug, she said, "I've something to show you. Fetch your hat and gloves. I'll wait for you outside."

"What is it? Where are we going?" I asked.

She grinned. "It's a surprise."

Pleased I'd be getting to spend some time with my friend, I ran up to my room, where I dropped off the parcel and selected my amethyst hat with the wide brim. I was putting it on with the mirror's guidance when my mother entered my room. A chilly air accompanied her. "I've always been partial to that hat," she said. She reached over to give it a stylish slant and tucked a tendril of hair neatly behind my ear. She then stepped back and scrutinized me, her countenance resting in the murky area between somewhat displeased and mildly satisfied. "It's a little large for going to market, though, don't you think." It was a statement, not a question.

Though my body was tense, I gave her as warm a smile as I could manage.

"I didn't realize that's where we are going," I said, making no movement to exchange it for a different hat. I pressed my fingernail into the palm of my hand, hoping she wouldn't forbid me from going with Claire. "I believe Claire was trying to keep it a secret."

"Yes, well, I spoke with Giles's coachman when he

first pulled up. So, surprise," she said flatly, waving her fingers in the air by my face.

"May I go?" I asked.

"You may."

"Thank you, Mother." She stood perfectly motionless while I kissed her cheek. I left her standing in my room, her head turned to gaze out the window. Though I was tempted to run down the stairs, I didn't want to give her any reason to change her mind about my going. So I held up my chin, pointed my toes, and ran my fingers lightly along the curves of the railing. Solomon was ready for me by that time and had the door open, and in turn, Giles's coachman helped me into the carriage.

"Have you ever been to the marketplace?" Claire asked when I sat opposite her. "That's where we're going."

I nodded, choosing not to let her know my mother had already spilled the beans, so to speak. "I have. It's been a long time, though. My mother typically sends Rainy or one of her children to do our shopping."

When I was younger, my father and I would go and catch an acrobat act or a puppet show. Once, he bought me a crown an old lady had woven out of daisies. I wore the crown with enthusiasm and pride, until my mother saw it and said, "What is that on your head, Regina? You look like a silly peasant girl." She'd reached over, plucked a single daisy petal, and flicked it into the air. The petal had performed a somber little dance, spiraling down, down, down to the floor. "One day, you will have a *real* crown," my mother had said, "one of gold and jewels."

"To the marketplace," Giles's coachman cried as he cracked the whip. I gave the front door one last look as we rolled away, half expecting my mother to appear and say she'd changed her mind. The greater the distance between the carriage and my house, the more at ease I felt.

Almost an hour later, as we crossed a bridge and got our first glimpse of the market stands and carts, I was struck by an array of wonderful smells—those of smoked pork and mutton, freshly baked bread, and buttery beans. My stomach growled as if it had been days since I'd filled it.

The coachman steered the carriage over to the side

of the road, where Claire and I stepped out and began making our way to the hustle and bustle of the marketplace. On the outskirts, a crippled man sat hunched on a tree stump, plucking out a joyful tune on a mandolin. I paused by his hat—a floppy black one with an assortment of patches—and tossed in a coin, which made the faintest *clink*. Without missing a note, he glanced up and gave me a crinkly wink and a gap-toothed grin.

Claire, who'd kept walking onward, came back to retrieve me, taking my arm in hers. "We must stick together," she said, sounding more like a mother to her child than a girl to her friend.

We meandered through the crowds of merchants and village children, occasionally sidestepping a skinny cat or a wayward hen. From time to time, Claire turned to look behind us. There was something about her—a distant, misty look in her eyes and a sheen of perspiration on her forehead—that worried me. "Claire, is somebody following us?" I asked, making her stop.

She wrung her hands. "What? No, I don't think so."

"Are you feeling well?"

She straightened her arms at her sides and blinked. "I sometimes get nervous in crowds, that's all. Oh, look. That must be the bread my uncle asked me to get for him."

A rotund man with a pointy beak of a nose hustled and bustled about as he peddled his bread. I joined Claire in the queue. When it was her turn to be helped, a boy with stringy red hair zipped by, snatching a loaf as he went. The baker ran after him at uncanny speed, given the size of his stomach. Realizing the baker was gaining on him, the boy threw the loaf in the opposite direction. A dozen meters away, the loaf lay discarded in the dirt. Not a second later, a pair of little girls picked it up and fled into a thicket.

I heard a squeal and looked up. The baker had pegged the redheaded urchin against the side of a stage where a juggler was performing. Or *had been* performing, as the juggler squealed some more and jumped off the stage, knocking a burly bearded man in the audience on the head with one of his wooden clubs. The bearded man wound up his arm and punched the juggler right in the gut, which sent the scrawny man careening into a gaggle of old ladies, one of whom had a calf on a rope. Punches were thrown and shouts and curses filled the air, and the newly freed calf scurried this way and that, trying to escape the chaos.

Meanwhile, the baker held the young thief by the scruff of his neck, giving him quite a beating. Between wallops, the boy whimpered and sobbed and promised he'd never steal again. But the baker kept pounding on him. Unable to watch a second longer, I stepped forward, but Claire held out her arm, restricting me. "What are you doing, Regina?"

When I looked at her, I noticed she again had that strange faraway look in her eye. "I have to stop him," I said. "He's hurting that boy. Maybe if I offer to pay for the bread, the baker will leave him alone."

"Stay here. I'll take care of it." Claire narrowed her eyes and lifted her right hand. Mashing her lips together, she made a low guttural noise. I was so puzzled by my friend's bizarre behavior, I didn't notice what had happened until one of the old ladies screamed, "Fire!" The bedlam instantly stopped, and everybody turned to see what the woman was yelling about.

The baker's boots were on fire! I looked between him and Claire as he hollered and hopped about, and she stood by me, glassy-eyed, until it finally dawned on me that *she*'d set his feet on fire.

Claire had *magic*?

The baker bounced over to a trough, scaring off the calf, which had been drinking from it. In one smooth movement, he leapt into the water, alternately praising the gods and cursing.

"Claire? How . . . How did you *do* that?" I asked when I found my voice.

By then, the villagers had begun eyeing those around them with overt curiosity. "Witch, show yourself!" someone demanded from the far side of the stage.

I grabbed my friend's arm and headed back in the direction of the bridge, where Giles's carriage would be waiting to bring us home. The unmanned bread stand came into view just in time for us to witness the red-headed boy swipe two more loaves and then scamper off, with a slight limp and the beginning of what would surely become a deep purple shiner.

"He'll continue to steal, but I have a feeling the baker won't be tempted to beat little boys anymore," Claire said once the carriage began rolling along the road, homebound.

I ignored that. "Why didn't you tell me you had magic?" I demanded instead.

Before Claire could respond, the carriage jostled to a halt. She hung her head out the window to ask the coachman, "What is going on? Why have we stopped?"

A moment later, he answered from the perch, "Apologies, Miss Claire. An old woman was in the way, chasing after a calf. We're all clear now, though."

"Very good," she said, and the horses commenced trotting down the road.

My patience was no match for my curiosity. "I can't believe you've had magic all this time and you never told me."

She cast her eyes downward. "I merely dabble in it from time to time."

"Dabble in it?" I repeated incredulously. "You set a man's boots aflame!"

She blinked several times. "I suppose I did."

"And yet, why didn't you use it when the blind witch attacked us?"

"The blind witch?" She twirled a strand of hair. "Oh. I really don't know."

"You didn't think of it?" I asked.

She swallowed and her gaze met mine. "I guess I didn't know if my magic would have had any impact."

Again, Claire was being too modest. However, if she didn't have enough power on her own, surely the pair of us would be a force to be reckoned with. Unable to check myself, I reached across the bench and took her hands in mine. Hers felt chilly, despite the agreeable weather. "You must teach me your magic," I said, my voice transparent with desperation.

"As you wish," she said. "Come over to my uncle's tomorrow."

I blinked. That hadn't been difficult. Claire wasn't the least bit reluctant. "Thank you, Claire," I said, fearing what I was about to say might sabotage my chances. However, I wouldn't feel right about taking her up on her generous offer without warning her. I took a deep breath and forged on. "My mother will not want me to learn. If she finds out you've agreed to teach me, she . . ." I flexed my jaw, not really knowing how to finish. "Let's just say she would not be amused."

"That's why we'll be careful. She'll never find out about the lessons, because she'll never know I have magic. I'm very good at keeping it a secret."

I felt giddy as the carriage swept past the orchard and up my drive, delivering me to my house. Now Claire and I had a secret between us, and it was a big one. I thanked the coachman and gave the horses each a gentle rub on their velvet-soft muzzles before heading inside.

Nine

"I've never been up here," I said as Claire and I climbed a narrow, winding staircase within her uncle's house. I'd scarcely slept the night before, as I was too wound up about learning magic. I'd ducked around my parents and the servants all day to keep them from noticing anything different about me. Soon Claire and I stood before a small arched door with a brass doorknob, and I held the candle up as steadily as possible so Claire could better see the keyhole. The lock gave a satisfying *click* and the door yawned open, screeching like a mad alley cat.

"This is where I come when I want to be alone," Claire said, her voice echoing against the stone walls.

Overhead, a moth fluttered recklessly along the rafters that peaked to form the pinnacle of Giles's house. "As you can see, my uncle stores Aunt Louise's belongings up here. Things he couldn't bear to get rid of—and yet, he never comes here, because seeing them brings him too much grief."

"I remember her," I said. "She'd accompany your uncle on his doctor visits and bring along her needlepoint and songs to entertain and cheer the patients' worried families. Whenever a woman gave birth to a baby girl, she'd give them a generous gift of hair ribbons. Everybody adored her."

One winter night, Louise went into labor. Giles had delivered many babies before, and he was thrilled to be bringing his own child into the world. However, there were complications. Somehow, his own wife died in childbirth, and their baby was stillborn. I'd never forget the snowy day we all dressed in black and gathered at the cemetery to bury both her and their infant boy in a single coffin. I didn't know if Giles had ever forgiven himself.

I lit a candelabrum on an old bureau, shedding more light and casting shadows on the furniture, shelves, pots, and chairs arranged on the wooden planked floor. I lifted a large tan cloth covering to reveal a precious wooden crib, carved with little bears and trees. Inside it was nothing but a folded blanket, its edges embroidered with matching bears. Shaking my head, I draped the cloth back over the baby bed. Next I opened the curtains on the lone window, trying to brighten not only the room, but the mood.

"My aunt Louise liked to write, and she kept journals." Claire gestured at a tall, narrow bookcase that held a dozen or so volumes. "Many of them are empty, so sometimes I come up here and write stories in them."

I ran my fingers along a row of leather-bound spines. "What kind of stories?" I couldn't help wondering if any of them were about me.

She shrugged. "I wrote one the day we picked the apple from your orchard."

"Really? How does it go?" I asked.

She rolled her shoulders back and stood tall. "When

a sailor would take off on a lengthy journey, his beloved would give him the first apple of the harvest. As long as their love remained pure as starlight, the apple would stay as perfect as when she'd first picked it. Then, upon the sailor's safe return, they would cut into the apple together, and its seeds would be in the shape of a star."

I smiled at her. "That's lovely, Claire. Very romantic."

Her eyes lit up. "I'm glad you like it." She dusted off and arranged a small table and two chairs. "Are you ready to learn magic, Regina?" she asked, gesturing at the empty seat across from her.

"Am I ever!" I exclaimed as I sat.

She reached for my hands and turned them palms up. Her eyes slowly shifted side to side, and she swallowed. She closed her eyes, took a deep breath, and told me to do the same. I did as instructed. "Clear your mind, Regina. All you should see is darkness. All you should hear is my voice."

"All right," I agreed.

"No, don't speak. I need you to concentrate on *my* voice, not yours."

"Oh, my apologies."

"Regina!" She sighed. "I will tell you when it's all right for you to talk."

I pantomimed squeezing my lips shut. I heard her take another deep breath: *inhale, exhale*. "Now, picture the sea at nighttime," she said. "Inky black water and waves capped in midnight blue. The full moon is a deep yellow, with gray clouds overlaying it like gauze."

After a brief pause, she continued. "The moon is turning orange. Now it is red. The redness pours into the ocean and bleeds into the sky. Everything you see is red: the sea, sky, and moon. Keep your eyes closed. I am going to ask you a question, and I want you to answer out loud and in full honesty. Regina, what emotion are you feeling?" she asked.

"Well, anger, I suppose."

"Anger is a very powerful emotion," Claire said, sounding pleased. "We can definitely work with that. I want you to concentrate on that feeling. Since this is your first lesson, I want you to remember something that *recently* happened that made you angry. If possible, focus on something you're still mad about. Nod when you're ready to proceed."

Memories swarmed my mind, a vast majority of which centered on my mother. Most recently, three days ago, when she'd sent me to my room and bolted the door.

"Picture it in detail," Claire said.

I closed my eyes tighter, and I felt a hint of a smile tugging on my lips as I recalled what a beautiful morning it had been.

I'd just had an exhilarating ride on Rocinante. But my horse and I weren't the only ones in a good mood. When I'd gone down to the stables early that morning, I'd caught Jesse humming as he mucked the stalls. Even the birds and butterflies seemed to be in good spirits as they fluttered and coasted about in the blue sky, celebrating the sunniest morning of the season so far.

Rocinante was galloping back to the stables when I veered off into the thick of the orchard and brought him to a halt. Leaning back in the saddle and placing my hands on his haunches, I tilted my head toward the sky and breathed in the sweetness of the dewy apple blossoms.

When I first spotted a red apple dangling from one of the highest branches, I blinked to make sure it wasn't a mirage caused by gazing into the direct sunlight. However, even after rubbing my eyes and guiding Rocinante a few steps to the side, it remained. Never had the orchard produced a single fruit in the springtime, let alone a ripe one. The way I figured it, the lone apple was a good three months early.

I had to have it.

I slid out of the saddle and tried to climb the tree, but the lowest branch was too high. After some trial and error, I stood in the saddle, which put me within fingertips' reach of the apple. Struggling to balance, I stretched higher and smiled when I grazed it.

I heard my mother call, "Regina! What in the land are you doing? Have you lost your mind?"

Cursing her for seeing me and myself for not having checked to make sure she was nowhere around, I carefully lowered myself down and sat sidesaddle. "Nothing, Mother. I was trying a new trick."

"A new trick? Did it not occur to you that you could have fallen and broken your neck? My magic can do many things, but it cannot bring you back from the dead."

"Yes, I know. I'm sorry, Mother. But as you can see, I'm

perfectly fine." I made an effort not to allow my gaze to drift to the apple. If I couldn't pick it right then, perhaps I could return for it later.

"What was that?" she asked, inclining her head like she hadn't heard me, even though she had the senses of a hawk.

"I'm truly sorry, Mother," I said, trying my best to sound like I meant it.

She crossed her arms over her chest. "Go to your room and think about how you're not to 'try new tricks' ever again," she said, as if I were a child.

Rocinante pawed at the earth. "I'll go, but first let me take him back to the stables."

"I will make sure your horse gets back to the stables. Now, go." She raised her hand, and using magic, tethered Rocinante to one of the trees. Poor Rocinante stomped and threw back his head, the whites of his eyes showing. To make matters worse, she'd given him hardly any wiggle room.

"Go to your room," my mother repeated. As I made my way back to the house, growing more furious with each step, I glanced back at Rocinante. Why was she punishing him? He'd done nothing

wrong. If anything, he'd held steady so that I didn't fall. Rocinante would never do anything to hurt me.

My mother's words replayed in my mind: Go to your room.

How dare *she. I was* sixteen, *not six! Even if she had caught me riding in perfect form on the sidesaddle, she still would have found something to criticize. Nothing I did was ever enough for her.*

I flung open the front door and stormed into the foyer. Solomon stood in the corner, moving only to close the door quietly yet firmly in my wake.

Out of the corner of my eye, I spied my father playing chess with Giles in the smoking room. I knew he saw me, too. He raised his head, but he did not stand. He just sat there, holding the queen piece in midair. It was as if time stood still, except for the anger flooding through me.

"Open your eyes, Regina." Claire's soft voice brought me out of my memory. I'd been so consumed by it that I'd forgotten where I was and whom I was with. I felt exhausted, physically and mentally.

"Slowly stand up."

Though my legs trembled, I did so.

"Good." Claire rose and walked around the table, stopping behind me. "Focus on the candles. Use that feeling of anger and extinguish them," she commanded, pointing at the seven dancing flames atop the old, dusty bureau.

It didn't work.

I quickly exhaled and then inhaled.

The flames flickered insolently. *Would it be enough to direct my anger to the candles, since they weren't cooperating?* But that was more frustration than anger, I thought.

"Visualize the candles being blown out one by one," Claire urged.

I envisioned it. Clenching my eyelids closed, I tried harder. Confidence filled me, coursing through my veins. The anger heated my blood and I felt it pass down my arms and out of my open palms.

The flame on the left side of the candelabrum seemed to dim, and I almost cheered with joy. However, my celebration would have been premature, for when I blinked to make sure, it was still lit. Had it been my imagination, my hope, playing tricks on me? I glanced down at my hands. There was no purple smoke like my mother made. No smoke at all.

When Claire looked at me, her eyes were wide.

"Don't pity me," I said softly.

"I don't," she replied. "I just . . . I don't understand why it's not working. Perhaps you simply need more practice." She pursed her lips and blew out the candle on the left.

"Yes, practice. I'm sure that's it," I said, rolling the crisp fabric of my blouse between my thumb and forefinger. On second thought, perhaps Claire's instruction was missing something important. Still, I didn't want to insult her by suggesting she was a less than adequate teacher, so I asked, "Is this how your first magic lesson went?"

"Oh. Well . . ." She sucked in her lower lip for a second or two. "We aren't supposed to reveal those things. You shouldn't make known what we do in our lessons, either. It's . . . how it is. We will try again tomorrow, after tea." She shrugged and then leaned over and blew out the remaining candles.

Ten

Tuesday, May 9

"Good morning, Regina," Jasper B. Holding said as he set up my paints and easel. He was correct; it was an exceptionally lovely morning. My shoes glistened with dew I'd picked up trekking across the grass. Puffs of bright white clouds dotted the cerulean sky, and though the sun shone brightly, the breeze kept me cool despite my decision to wear my hair down.

"Good morning, Jasper. I brought something for you," I said, desperately trying to hide the blush that I felt creeping over my cheeks.

He situated the wooden stools and peered up at me

through his reddish-brown hair. His hair was longer on top, and had an endearing way of flopping into his blue-green eyes even when there was no wind to blame. I wanted to run my fingers through it, but the mere thought of doing so made my palms sweat.

"What is it?" he asked. He sounded wary, perhaps even frightened.

Inwardly, I sighed. I wished he knew that even though I was Cora's daughter, he didn't have to fear me.

But I had to confess, I also liked how I could put him on edge.

"A surprise," I said. "Close your eyes."

Jasper tucked his hands into the pockets of his trousers and glanced up at the house and then back at me. Finally, he took a quick breath and shut his eyes.

"Hold out your hand." He did so, and I placed the apple in it. "All right, open up."

He stared down at the apple, which I'd polished to a nearly blinding gleam. "It's an apple," he said, his tone rising at the end as if in question.

"Do you notice anything *special* about this one?" I

asked, having gotten enough confidence back to do so coyly.

"It's very nice," he said. "Especially for this time of year."

"Yes," I agreed. "Would you go so far as to say it's *perfect?*"

He grinned, but I could tell he still had no idea what the deeper meaning was. "Yes, I would. In fact, it would be a shame to eat such a fine example of fruit."

"Ah! But, if you recall, you said, 'Nothing found in nature is truly perfect.'" I placed my finger on the apple, silently driving my point into his mind for a second or two. "It was when I painted tree trunks perfectly straight, and the leaves perfectly symmetrical. That was the context."

He laughed, his eyes dancing. "And you brought me this apple so I could literally eat my words?"

"I could never have passed up such a *perfect* opportunity," I said.

A breeze blew past, sweeping my hair into my eyes. I brushed it off my face as best I could. Jasper reached over and gently ran his thumbnail along my brow to get the strands that had stuck in my lashes. "Thank you," I said. Yet I couldn't look at him, not with the humiliating blush I felt staining my cheeks. Instead, I sat in the little wooden chair, crossed my ankles, and gripped my brush. "Now then, what shall I paint today?" I asked as glibly as possible, awestricken that with a simple gesture, Jasper had rendered me completely powerless. But unlike when my mother did so, this felt . . . pleasant. I dipped my brush in bright red and began painting. Before I knew it, I was caught up in my work.

"Regina?" he asked. I'd been so lost in my thoughts, I had no inkling whether minutes or hours had passed.

I looked up from my painting.

"When I said nothing in nature is truly perfect, I was mistaken." He looked at me deeply, like he had when he was painting my portrait. I felt his eyes linger on each of my features in turn, as if committing them to memory. Though my instinct was to fidget under his perusal, I forced myself to sit still. "Since then, I've learned perfection does occur in nature, but only once in a great while." His gaze lingered on my lips, and I turned my head. A horrible heat rose to my face, no doubt turning it the same hue as the apple in his hand.

"How was your art lesson?" my mother asked between sips of her tea. I kept waiting for the announcement that Claire was there to call on me, but teatime seemed to drag on for an eternity.

"It was fine, Mother."

Keeping secrets from my mother was tough business, and I tried not to squirm or give her any reason to suspect I might be pining for my art teacher. Or that I had an inkling he might possibly feel the same way about me.

"What are you and Casper working on now?"

I sloshed the steaming tea in my cup, bringing it precariously close to the rim. It didn't taste as sweet as usual, and I couldn't help wondering if Rainy was under strict orders to put less sugar on the table now that party season was on the horizon.

"Jasper," I said.

"What's that?"

"My art teacher's name is *Jasper.*"

"Oh."

"I'm painting a landscape of the apple orchard."

"That sounds nice." The corner of her mouth ticked upward for a split second, almost looking like a smile.

"Would you like to see it?" I asked. "It isn't finished, but it's close. I'm sure you can get the idea, anyhow."

"You needn't babble, Regina." She rang the bell, and Solomon entered the room.

"Yes, Your Highness?"

"Bring us Regina's painting," my mother said.

"It's the one of the orchard, next to my wardrobe."

She sipped her tea as we waited for his return, but my belly was twisted in knots. When Solomon held up my painting for my mother to scrutinize, I felt like a desperate little girl. I wanted nothing more than to hear my mother's praise. When her lips parted to speak, I clasped my hands in my lap and held my breath.

"Well, we cannot be good at everything," she said, shooing Solomon, and my painting, out.

Under the table, I pressed my fingernails into the soft centers of my palms. "No, I suppose we cannot."

Later, when I was reading in the library to pass the time, Solomon came in and announced Claire's arrival. I hurried out to the foyer and greeted my friend with a hug.

"What do you two girls have planned this afternoon?" my mother asked, entering the foyer behind us. The second Claire saw her, she let go of me and instead stood at my side.

"We haven't any plans," I said, shrugging. "At least, nothing interesting." Keeping my feelings for Jasper hush-hush was hard enough; now I had to keep Claire's magic lessons secret, as well.

Claire cleared her throat. "I've invited Regina to my uncle's house. She has such beautiful penmanship, and I would like for her to help me write my mother a special letter, as it's almost her birthday. If that is acceptable to you, of course."

My mother beamed. "It is fine with me, Claire."

Although I simply wanted to slip out without raising

any suspicions, a wave of irritation hit me. *Why is everything Claire suggests always a good idea?* I mashed my lips together, determined not to take it out on my friend. It wasn't her fault. And really, shouldn't I be thankful my mother wasn't doing everything in her power to sabotage our relationship?

My mother smoothed what must have been a flyaway tress behind my ear and added, "It's a thoughtful gesture, and I'm certain your mother will be deeply touched by it." She glanced at me but didn't meet my eyes. "I don't believe my own daughter has ever written me anything."

I shifted my weight from one leg to the other.

"Oh. Well, thank you, Cora," Claire said, breaking the tension. "I do hope you're right and my ma likes it."

My mother laughed. Claire might have interpreted it as a jovial, carefree chuckle. But I knew better. "Oh, my dear girl," she said, laughing once more. "I am *always* right."

Instead of bringing us to Giles's house as expected, the white carriage delivered us to a small frog pond in the woods just beyond it. After Claire told the coachman when to come back for us, she sat on a moss-covered log on the bank and patted the space next to her.

"I cannot thank you enough for teaching me," I said, hoping to get the session started on a positive note. "I have a feeling I'll make progress today." I took a seat next to her and held on to my knees.

"Yes, I'm sure you will, Regina."

As I looked around, a sense of serenity filled my heart. *If the place woven into my bedroom rug really existed,* I thought, *this might be it.* Lily pads floated on the deep green water, some bearing white and yellow flowers, and one carrying a rather plump and vocal bullfrog. Glittery dragonflies, delicate butterflies, and a variety of birds populated the air and shoreline. They all went on with their lives, seemingly undisturbed by the two human trespassers.

"Do you see that frog on the lily pad?" Claire asked.

I nodded. "I spotted him right when I sat down. Hard to miss, as big as he is."

"Good. He's your target today."

"You mean, kill him?"

She crinkled her nose. "Or just make him fall into the water."

She guided me through the energy-centering exercises again. I brewed up all my anger and concentrated on the frog. *Fall into the water.* The command resonated in my mind so clearly, so loudly, so fully; I could think of no excuse for it not to happen.

The frog flicked out his tongue and ate a fly. He blinked his big yellow eyes, and though I couldn't tell from a distance, I could have sworn he had the nerve to let out a most indulgent belch.

I gawked at the impudent creature, feeling like I was the one falling into the pond, with stones tied to my feet. Sinking down, down, down. My lungs running out of air. My heart running out of hope.

No. I wouldn't allow myself to be without hope.

I set my jaw and held out my hand, forcing the heat in my body to concentrate in my open palm. I focused on the frog so intensely I thought I might have screamed out loud.

Then the frog was in the pond water. I'd blinked at a most unfortunate time, so I couldn't know with certainty how it had happened. Still, the frog was no longer on the lily pad. Wide-eyed, I looked at my friend. "Was that . . . ?"

Claire's grin spread from ear to ear. "Magic? Yes, my friend, I believe it was."

As I embraced Claire and celebrated my success, I wondered what my mother would do if she were here to see me doing magic for the first time.

Directly behind us, the grass rustled. Claire twisted around and screamed. A second later, I got a glimpse of what had her so panicked.

"It's just a snake," I said in a chiding tone. But I had to confess I was glad when it slithered away and out of sight under a moss-speckled boulder.

Eleven

Tuesday, May 16

Claire gave me magic lessons almost every day, and when she couldn't I practiced on my own. However, it had been an entire week and I hadn't made any more progress. "You're doing fine, Regina," she'd insisted. "Magic can't be rushed."

My friend's encouraging, patient words had been drowned out by a voice in my head. It kept questioning whether the frog flopping into the water had anything to do with my emerging magic, or if he'd simply hopped off the lily pad of his own volition. Any confidence I'd accrued was slipping through my fingers like sand.

My mounting stress caused me a disagreeable stomach, and the previous night, I'd had a disturbing nightmare.

In it, I knelt beside Jasper, who lay in the green grass of a vast meadow. Though he appeared to be dead, his chest rose and fell just enough to confirm he was merely sleeping. I leaned over and kissed his lips, then waited for his eyes to flutter open. A horrible laugh filled the air, and I glanced up to see my mother dressed in a sleek black jacket and high heels. Before I could ask her what she was doing there, she disappeared in a cloud of smoke, leaving behind a perfect red apple. When I picked up the apple, I saw someone had taken a bite out of it. The apple started glowing and beating in my hand, morphing into a heart. It turned from red to black and, finally, to nothing but dust.

The nightmare had been so realistic, I was actually brushing my palms together when I awoke, trying to wipe off the blackish-red residue.

Although I'd spent a good ten minutes staring at my reflection in my bedroom mirror, trying to rise above the malaise and put my best face forward for Jasper, I kept thinking I should have stayed under the covers and told Rainy I wasn't feeling well.

Then again, she would have alerted my parents, and before I knew it, Giles would've been at our home, pressing down my tongue with a spoon and making me say *aaaaaaah*. When he couldn't find anything wrong with me, he'd probably make me take some kind of terrible-tasting medicine anyway, to appease my mother.

"Uh-oh," Jasper said, raising his brows at me as I made my way over to the easel and chairs he'd set up by the orchard for that day's lesson.

Uh-oh? I suddenly wondered if, in my disheartened state, I'd forgotten to do something important, like button up my blouse. However, after a quick check, I seemed to be adequately put together. Besides, Rainy would not have allowed me out of the house had I not been. "What is it, Jasper?"

"You look like your dog died. He didn't, did he?"

"No. Thaddeus is alive and as fine as can be expected.

Although, he's so lazy, sometimes I wonder if he's been put under a sleeping spell."

"I'm glad to hear he's well. I grew rather fond of that hound when I painted your family portrait. I've never had anyone—person or pet—sit so still for the entire process. Or snore so loudly."

I shook my head at the joint memory, and I felt my spirits rising.

"Now, speaking of portraits, that's a good way to think about painting landscapes," Jasper said. "Paint every tree, every blade of grass, every cloud as if each is a person with its own unique characteristics."

As he began detailing the day's goals, I lost myself in a daydream. In it, Jasper brushed my hair off my face and gazed longingly into my eyes. *What are you thinking about, Regina?* he asked. From under my lashes, I gazed at him coyly and asked if he would paint my portrait—just me, this time. *I will, if that's what you wish,* he responded. *However, I'll never be able to fully capture your true beauty with mere paint.* His face moved nearer to mine, and I closed my eyes and—

"So, do you have all of that?" Jasper asked, and I blinked out of my fantasy. He grinned so charmingly, I couldn't help smiling back, just a little.

"Ah, that's better," he said, clapping his hands together twice. "You should smile more often. Now, sit. You have a painting to finish. I have a feeling this will be your best one yet, Regina."

I sighed inwardly. Jasper always dedicated every minute of our time together to art lessons, nothing more. "Must we paint today, Jasper?" I asked.

"Do you want to use another medium?"

"No. I mean, how about we . . . I don't know, go on a horseback ride? Or maybe we could take a stroll to the meadow?"

He pinched the bridge of his nose. "Regina, when I'm here, it's to teach you how to paint. It's what your parents hired me to do. While going on a ride or walk with you sounds pleasant, I'm afraid I cannot." His gaze shifted from my face—which I tried to keep neutral so he wouldn't see how disappointed and embarrassed I was about being turned down—to the house. I was sure he thought my mother was watching us from the balcony, and he was probably correct. Now that I thought about it, she'd probably made him vow to keep all the painting lessons within sight of the house, as they all had been and likely would forever be. I gritted my teeth, frustrated.

If only Jasper and I could meet sometime on the sly and spend some time together beyond the art lessons. Someplace where my mother wasn't able to watch our every move. I was suddenly struck with an idea.

"Jasper, are you attending King Leopold and Queen Eva's ball Saturday evening?" I asked. Normally, this would be a very rude question, since artists were rarely, if ever, on the guest list for royal functions. However, the king and queen had hired Jasper to paint their portraits and had recommended him highly to my parents, so I believed there was a chance they'd made an exception.

"I received an invitation," he answered. "I thought it might be a good place to meet prospective clients."

My heart leapt. "Wonderful. You should definitely go, then. I will be there."

"I thought you might." Neither his expression nor his tone gave me a hint as to whether he was happy about that or not.

I took a deep breath, smiled broadly, and decided to be optimistic. "Well, I do hope to see you there. If you decide to attend, I believe that at ten o'clock I'll have become weary of all the music and dancing and need to wander outside." I brainstormed someplace to meet as quickly as I could, recalling one of my favorite spots to ride Rocinante, especially in the spring and summer. "There's a lovely little bridge just beyond the rose garden, the perfect place to get some fresh air. Perhaps you'll need some fresh air, as well."

He cocked his right eyebrow. "I think I know your parents well enough to say they wouldn't be keen on us meeting up outside of your lessons," he said, sounding frustratingly logical.

"They would never find out," I said. "I promise. It will be our secret, and even if we are caught, I'll say it was happenstance we were in the same place at the same time, and insist to my parents I didn't want to be impolite by ignoring my art teacher."

He looked at me for a long while before sighing as if in surrender. "Very well then. I will meet you at this bridge you speak of."

"Ten o'clock," I reminded him, much too eagerly.

"At the stroke," he agreed.

I was very much looking forward to going to the ball. Not only would Claire be there, but now, so would Jasper. I wasn't quite sure what we would do once he and I were on the bridge, but the thought of outfoxing my mother—even in this small way—brought a smile to my face.

With that, Jasper started on my lesson, and I resigned myself to focusing on my painting. Then I realized Jasper's gaze had again drifted away. I turned my head in time to see him focusing on Giles's white carriage as it came creeping up the drive. My father had mentioned over breakfast he would be coming by.

"Looks like you have company," Jasper said.

"It's a friend of my father's." But then Claire stepped out of the carriage, too. "And his niece, who happens to be my dear friend. Rainy will see to her. She can wait in the library until we are finished," I said, knowing my mother would prefer that arrangement so I could get the most out of my lesson.

"Nonsense. I will gather her," Jasper offered. "She can sit in my chair and keep you company while you paint."

A few minutes later, Jasper and Claire were meandering around a patch of wildflowers. My friend wore a simple frock the color of a robin's egg, and it made her eyes appear even brighter than usual. I smiled and waved, but to my disappointment, she must not have seen me.

Frowning, I realized why I wasn't as happy about Claire's visit as I normally would have been. My time with Jasper was short and precious, and yes, I could admit I wanted him all to myself.

Claire was giggling. I'd heard her laugh countless times, and yet, curiously, it had never sounded so light and melodic before. Had Jasper told her a joke? I wondered. If so, was he going to tell it to me, too? She stooped to pick a flower and tucked it into the braid that crowned her head, which made her look even prettier and sweeter.

I waved again, and this time she waved back. After we wished each other a good morning, Claire said, "I was just telling Jasper how much I admire the portraits he painted of your family. By the by, Regina, you told me all about Jasper, but you failed to mention how handsome he is."

I tightened my grip on the paintbrush as mortification set in. I had told her *all about Jasper*? She was making it sound like I was in love with him. Which I most certainly was *not*, and even so, I surely didn't want Jasper to know in this pathetic way. And *how handsome he is*? What was going on? Could it be that my best friend was flirting with my art teacher? There was no denying he was reveling in her attention, the way he chuckled softly and his cheeks reddened. I felt my own face heat up, too, but not from bashfulness. I felt something deep inside of me snap like a twig.

"You'll have to pardon my friend," I said to Jasper. "Apparently young women who live in port towns are quite forthright."

Claire's eyes widened as if she'd been slapped, and she shrank away from us. "It's true, my tongue sometimes gets the better of me. I apologize for my bluntness." She drew her bottom lip through her teeth, appearing rather small and awkward as she stood there. She was the portrait of a maiden in distress, and I had begun feeling guilty for how I'd treated her when Jasper came to her rescue.

He gestured for Claire to take the chair in which he usually sat, and made a big to-do about ensuring her comfort. "No harm done," he said. "Sometimes I wish more people would speak plainly."

I smiled at both of them, but I was bearing down on my back teeth. If Jasper wanted me to speak plainly, I could say I wished the two of them wouldn't flirt. Didn't they know they were making a spectacle of themselves?

"I suppose if *I'm* speaking plainly, I . . ." Claire and Jasper were looking at me with tilted heads, obviously waiting for me to finish my thought.

I faced Claire. "I wonder if you wouldn't mind waiting in the library until my lesson is finished. I'll find it easier to concentrate on my painting."

"Oh," she said, clearly taken aback by my request. "Of course, Regina. I understand." She stood, bowed her head, and took a few steps in the direction of my house. "It was nice to make your acquaintance, Jasper."

"I'm sure our paths will cross again," he called.

They're merely being civil, I told myself. What I'd witnessed was an ordinary exchange between people who'd recently been introduced and were parting ways. Still, I couldn't help noticing that although Jasper had turned his attention back to me, he was keeping half an eye on Claire as she walked away, her straw-colored hair blowing in the breeze. Again, it felt like something had snapped inside of me.

I gazed up at Jasper through my lashes. "If I'm speaking plainer still, I should confess I've forgotten the technique you taught me last week for painting grass. Would you mind showing me again?"

"By all means," he agreed, handing me a special brush with fanned-out bristles. "Start at the root and flick your wrist as you come up each blade of grass."

"Yes, but can you *show* me?" I reached out and lightly touched his arm.

He blinked a couple of times and then nodded. "Certainly. Here." He knelt behind me and reached around my right shoulder, cupping my hand in his. He moved my hand, he the puppeteer and I the marionette, creating wispy green brushstrokes on the canvas. I felt his chest pressing against the back of the chair, his breath in my hair. The air caught in my lungs. I wanted to tell him I remembered now so he would stop. I swallowed, afraid that if I uttered any words, they would come out unintelligible.

Suddenly, Jasper dropped my hand. The brush fell to the ground as if wounded. At first I thought he'd somehow read my mind. But when I looked up, I saw for myself what was the matter.

My mother was at the edge of the orchard, striding

toward us. With violet-colored vapors at her spiked heels, her hands on her hips, and her eyes blazing, it was clear she had seen us even before she spoke. "*What* are you doing with my daughter?"

Jasper scrambled to his feet, slipping as if he were skating on a frozen pond. "I was just . . ." He paused to clear his throat, and yet his voice still sounded like a frog's. "I was demonstrating how to do a special painting technique."

My mother raised her chin, and I froze in place. "I see. As far as I'm concerned, you've 'demonstrated' your 'technique' to Regina for the last time."

"Mother!" I stood on shaky legs, accidentally knocking my painting to the ground. "Allow me to explain."

My mother ignored me, training her glare on Jasper. A chilly air descended upon us, making me shiver. "Leave this instant," she said. "If you ever set foot on our estate again, you will be sorry." With that, she spun on her heels and walked up to the house as Claire had done a few minutes prior. As the cruel words I'd said about

Claire reverberated in my head, a lump the size of an apple formed in my throat, blocking the air from my lungs. I swallowed it down, realizing that had she not come in the first place, and had she not been so loose-lipped, I never would have felt the need to manipulate Jasper in such a way.

Though Jasper had recently been so close I'd felt his breath on my neck, now he might as well have been realms away. He didn't even bother to meet my gaze when he leaned my painting against a tree.

"Jasper, I'm sorry," I said softly. As he walked toward his cart—a rebuked dog with his tail tucked between his legs—I called after him, "I'll speak with my mother and make her see it was all a misunderstanding. Will I still see you Saturday night?" I realized how desperate I sounded, but I did not care. "Jasper!"

As he disappeared down the road, my mind reeled. I'd all but forced him to overstep the student-teacher line he'd so mindfully drawn at our very first lesson. Not to mention the line my mother had drawn the day I was born—between me and anyone who could potentially stand in the way of my becoming the queen.

Could anything I said to my mother actually make a difference? She wouldn't even need to resort to magic to blast Jasper into a world of hurt. A simple accusation whispered at a party would ensure he was never again commissioned by the Enchanted Forest's most affluent families.

It might not alter Jasper's fate, but I had to at least attempt to clear things up with my mother. The sooner the better.

Twelve

I ran into the house and nearly tripped over Thaddeus before finally tracking down my mother in the drawing room. With perfect posture and a serene countenance, she sat in the tapestry-upholstered, high-backed chair as if she were posing for a portrait by an invisible artist.

I stole a few seconds to catch my breath and gather as much composure as possible, given the fear that festered in my heart. I cleared my throat and pulled back my shoulders. "I apologize for interrupting you, Mother. I need to explain what you saw down by the orchard."

"You needn't waste any more of my time. I am quite certain what I saw. There is nothing wrong with my eyes."

"It wasn't Jasper's fault," I said miserably. "I asked him to show me a brushstroke, and he only did as I requested."

She exhaled loudly and crossed her arms. "I hired him to teach you how to paint, not to grope you with his paint-stained hands. His behavior was reprehensible."

"It wasn't like that, Mother. Truly."

"So, you're telling me you threw yourself at your art teacher, like a desperate little wench? Because if you are, you're saying you are willingly throwing away all the hard work I've put into making sure you become a queen." She arched an eyebrow as I struggled with my response.

"Well, I wouldn't say *that*."

She unfolded her arms and pointed a bejeweled finger at me. "Good. We are in agreement, then." She abruptly stood and began walking toward the doorway. Thaddeus bustled past in the direction of the living room as fast as his legs would carry him. "Jasper's fate is sealed."

"I will not leave until you've given me the opportunity to explain," I said, planting my feet firmly in front of her.

"Can't you step back and see that perhaps you've wanted to fire him all along, and you were looking for an excuse to do so?" As the words gushed out of my mouth, I realized how much truth they held. If she told my father what she saw—the scene I'd so recklessly orchestrated to prove to Claire, Jasper, and even myself that Jasper harbored romantic feelings for me—my father would undoubtedly be on board with her decision to dismiss him.

"I've heard quite enough from you, Regina." My mother narrowed her eyes and waved her hand. I covered my ears and steeled myself as best I could for whatever terrible magic she had in store for me. When nothing happened, I lowered my hands and exhaled in relief. Then I felt a featherlight sensation around my middle.

The sash that had been tied around my waist loosened. After floating before my eyes for a second or two, it snapped straight and wrapped itself over my mouth and around my head. I tried to protest, but my words were muted before they formed. When I began to unknot the sash, my fingers stuck to it. I could only imagine how ridiculous I looked, with my eyes bugging out and my hands glued to the back of my skull, hopelessly restrained.

Well, perhaps not hopelessly.

I had one last hope. Magic.

Drawing from what Claire had taught me so far, I concentrated on how it felt to be silenced in such a humiliating, infuriating manner. It didn't require much effort to conjure up those emotions, for they were at the forefront, the driving force behind every beat of my heart. It felt as if there were a ball of fire within my rib cage, scorching my insides. How desperately I needed it out of me! But not until I'd gleaned its power.

My mother selected a book from the shelf and started flipping through its pages, completely ignoring me. Hot tears sprang to my eyes, and it seemed I was seeing her through a pane of glass as red as the perfect apple I'd given Jasper. A noise rose from the depths of my throat, the guttural growl of a wild beast.

The smug look on my mother's face as she read—the upward quirk of her mouth and her laughing eyes—gave me the final amount of anger I needed. Closing my eyes and pressing my fingers into the back of my skull, I focused all of my power on removing the gag from my mouth. I could almost feel the sweet sensation of the sash slipping off, swirling as it floated down to the marble floor. How I yearned to see the look of utter shock on my mother's face when she realized I'd used magic.

She slipped the book back onto the shelf, and I felt the gag squeeze my jaw and ears like a corset. *Had I made that happen, or was it my mother's magic?* Perspiration coated my skin and my entire body shook uncontrollably. Suddenly, my knees gave out. A mere second before I surely would have toppled to the floor, my hands were freed, allowing me to reach out for the chair and break my fall.

"Are you quite all right, Regina?" my mother asked as if I'd merely stubbed my toe.

I couldn't bear to look up at her. Blinking hard, I willed the tears to stop streaming from my eyes, soaking the sash that remained tied around my head.

Fortunately, she didn't wait for me to answer. Perhaps that was because I couldn't speak, even if I'd wanted to. Her heels hammered along the floor as she stepped around me and exited the drawing room. I didn't lift my eyes until her footfalls sounded like a mere tapping in a distant hall.

Once I righted my posture, I was surprised to see I wasn't alone. Claire lingered outside the doorway, clutching my painting of the apple orchard. I wanted to know how long she'd been there, how much she'd witnessed. However, judging by the pallor of her face and the trembling of her lower lip, it was evident she'd seen plenty.

"Sorry," she said softly, her eyes resting uneasily on my gag. "I just . . . Well, I thought you might want this. You need to finish the grass. As I'm sure you know. Here," she said, putting the painting down, "let me help you."

As she reached out, the sash slipped off my face. It swirled as it floated down to the marble floor, exactly as I'd envisioned it doing earlier. However, the sensation was much more bitter than sweet. "Thank you, Claire," I said with my last shred of dignity. "I'm sorry you had to see that."

Interrupting the awkward moments that followed, Rainy burst into the room, balancing a silver tray stacked with dishes. "Oh, my!" she cried, setting the tray on the table with little grace. "I thought you were still in your lesson, Regina. It's not too blustery, is it?" she asked, drawing back the drapes and peering outside.

Claire came to the rescue with a story. "Jasper had an engagement. Regrettably, he was forced to cut Regina's lesson short."

Rainy's freckled, rounded cheeks puffed in and out. "Tsk, tsk. Your mother will not be pleased with such unprofessional behavior." Next she turned her attention to Claire. "I hope you'll be joining us for tea, dear. I've whipped up something special for today."

I wondered if she'd stay, given the way I'd treated her. To be honest, I was surprised she was still there. She glanced over at me, and I gave her a wee nod.

Claire's pretty face broke out into a grin, and she picked up my painting again. "In that case, how can I refuse?"

"Good. You two girls go freshen up, and I'll have everything ready at the stroke of two."

"I'll meet you in my room in a few minutes," I told Claire, and once she was on her way up the stairs, I took a quick detour to the dining hall, where I immediately noticed the family portrait Jasper had painted had been replaced by a tapestry depicting a fox hunt and a large silver-framed mirror. I wasn't surprised she'd abolished all evidence of Jasper in our home, yet I couldn't believe she'd gotten to it so quickly.

I balled up the sash and flung it into the fireplace. I'd always hated wearing sashes, tied up in big ridiculous bows. I only wore them because they pleased my mother. As the sash smoked and turned black, I watched with a mixture of satisfaction and fear. Once it disappeared altogether in the embers, I wiped away more tears I hadn't even realized I'd cried, took a deep breath, and then hurried up to my bedroom.

After what had happened with my mother, I could think of nothing more insufferable than sitting across from her, sipping tea. However, knowing Claire would be there made it more palatable.

I needed to apologize. Maybe that was why she hadn't gone. I really hadn't had much practice in apologies. Although, seeing her standing on the far side of my bedroom, my painting of the apple trees in her hands, I realized I didn't want to lose her. "Claire, back by the orchard, I . . ." I closed the door behind me, struggling to form the words. "I don't know what got into me. Something just . . . snapped."

Claire bowed her head graciously. "I owe you an apology, too. I truly had no idea you had feelings for Jasper."

"I don't."

She handed me the painting. "You're a mediocre painter and a horrid liar."

I laughed. "Okay, first off, this painting isn't even finished. Who knows? It might be brilliant . . . someday.

Secondly, you're right. I confess, I might feel a certain fondness toward Jasper. You know as well as I that my mother would never allow, let alone endorse, a courtship between him and me."

"That's true." I waited a moment to see if she'd say something more—maybe something romantic, to the effect that I shouldn't allow my mother to dictate my love life. However, she simply flopped onto my bedspread, wordlessly.

I stowed the painting among all my others in the back corner against the wall. I ran my finger over Rocinante's muzzle in the first picture I'd painted. It had only been three months since I'd met Jasper and started my lessons with him, and yet it felt like much longer. For the first time, the idea of having no more lessons settled in, and my heart dropped.

"Jasper is going to the ball on Saturday," I said. "I asked him to meet me at the rose bridge in the royal gardens at ten o'clock. He said he would, but that was before my mother fired him. Do you think there's a chance he'll still be there?"

"I don't think it would be wise. Your mother has made it very clear she doesn't want him anywhere near you."

"Well," I said, trying not to get discouraged by Claire's apparent need to be the voice of reason, "I was hoping I could get a little help from you. Like, maybe you can make sure my mother is engaged and doesn't realize I've left the ballroom at ten o'clock. That way, I can at least run out and check to see if he's there." If he was, it would prove he cared for me enough to take the risk. Further, it would be a victory for me over my mother—a victory she would never know about, but that would stay with me for all time. "Will you do that for me, Claire?"

"I will."

"Thank you, my friend," I said, lying next to her. I tucked one hand under my head and rested the other on her arm. "I'm so happy my mother brought you to live with your uncle."

"She didn't hurt you, did she?" Claire asked in such a low whisper I barely heard. She rolled onto her side, facing me. I turned my head to see her bright blue eyes soften with concern.

"She wouldn't even let me explain. I tried to use my own magic. I did everything you've taught me, Claire. I thought it was working, truly I did. But I failed. I failed spectacularly." I grabbed a pillow from overhead and pressed it onto my face.

"You didn't fail," she said, peeling the pillow off me and tossing it aside. "You're not ready to do that kind of magic, that's all."

When *would* I be ready? Things were only getting worse, and the last thing I wanted to hear was that I wasn't ready. I rolled onto my side, turning my back to Claire.

"I know it's not what you want to hear, Regina, and I'm sorry. But I'll help you through it. I promise."

"Really?"

Maybe Claire was right. Perhaps I should wait a while and see what happened. Maybe she was right that I hadn't failed. After all, I'd finally stood up to my mother. Although it probably had done nothing to make things right with Jasper, and my mother's magic had been more humiliating and agonizing than ever before, I'd survived.

I flopped over to my back, and together we stared up into my canopy.

I'd survived, and I had my best friend at my side.

"Regina," she said, "I have the feeling you'll be a force to be reckoned with someday."

Thirteen

"How nice that you could join us," my mother greeted Claire as she took a seat in the drawing room. Whether she was truly glad to have company or not, I could not tell. It never ceased to amaze and sicken me how she could act like a perfect family lived within these walls.

"Thank you for having me, Cora," Claire replied. She sat as if against a sharp sword, like any wiggle or bend of her spine might cause it to slice into her flesh.

"It's our pleasure. I'm sure your uncle is enjoying having you under his roof. Speaking of Giles," my mother said, "I hope he isn't making many calls. It's finally party season, and I'd hate to hear any terrible sicknesses or plagues are going around."

"None I know of," Claire said. "Most of his calls of late are just breech births and unpleasant stomach issues." Her eyes widened and she quickly added, "I apologize if those topics are unsuitable while at the table."

My mother arched one of her eyebrows. "Don't be silly, Claire. No topic is unsuitable at this table. Unless, of course, it's one I don't care to discuss." She chuckled softly, making it seem like a little joke, but I knew it to be the truth, and I suspected Claire did, too.

In the moments that followed, with the only noises being of our breathing and the delicate *ting-ting*s of stirring spoons, my mother gave me a sideways glance. "Regina, you're being quiet." She blotted her dark red lips with one of the monogrammed napkins she'd had imported in spite of the way my father's face blanched whenever she spent exorbitant amounts of money on such things. "Have you anything to contribute to our conversation?" she asked.

Actually, I do. Should I wait so you can use your magic to gag me first? As you can see, I'm not wearing a sash, but maybe a napkin will suffice? I hadn't said the words out loud, but the amused look on my mother's face made me wonder if her magic included mind reading. Suddenly, Claire wasn't the only one sitting at the table with extremely rigid posture.

"I have nothing to contribute at this time, Mother," I said, trying to appear more comfortable and confident than I felt.

My mother offered me one of Rainy's fine biscuits, loaded with almonds, raisins, and cinnamon, and smiled. It was such a kindhearted smile; I felt my stomach plummet. "My dear daughter, I'm sure Claire would agree releasing your art teacher was the only respectable choice in the matter. What kind of mother would I be if I allowed him to touch you as if you were a waitress in a seedy tavern?"

Claire made the smallest noise, like a faint hiccup, and she held her teacup to her lips without sipping. Claire's mother owned a tavern. And, as Claire confessed when we'd first met, she'd been well on her way to becoming a lifelong tavern girl herself, had she not come to live with her uncle. My mother's insensitive words stabbed Claire in the chest, and my heart went out to my friend.

"Mother." My voice wavered, and so I banged my fist on the table to keep my nerves from getting the best of me. "How could you say such a thing? Claire is my friend. She's the best friend I've ever had. Do you mean to push her away, the way you have with everyone else who's shown any interest in me whatsoever?"

"Goodness, Regina. Compose yourself this instant. I wasn't speaking of Claire. How quickly you forget *I* was once a tavern girl."

I hated to admit it, even to myself, but she was right. My mother *had* been a tavern waitress when she was younger, and I'd been so bent on accusing her of trying to sabotage my friendship that I'd rashly jumped to the wrong conclusion.

"*You* were a tavern girl?" Claire asked my mother, and

I couldn't blame her for failing to hide her shock. To look at Cora now—perfectly poised, stylishly coiffed and dressed, and calling one of the kingdom's most luxurious estates home—one would never have guessed she'd had such a modest beginning.

Her father, my grandfather, had been a miller. In his day, she'd told me, he'd run a simple yet successful business milling wheat into flour and delivering it not only to the villagers, but to King Xavier himself. However, by the time my mother was about my age, my grandfather had become a "lazy drunkard," and had she not taken work at the local pub, they both would have starved. She'd worked hard, but in her heart of hearts, my mother knew she was destined to be more than a miller's daughter or a waitress in a tavern.

"It's true," I said in a small voice.

"It seems like a lifetime ago," my mother said. "Perhaps it was. At any rate, I know firsthand the reprehensible ways men treat a woman in that position. They'll rub their grubby hands all over her body, leaving their stink on her—one that stays on her skin even after the longest and hottest of baths." She shuddered at the memories, and I saw Claire tremble, too. "Worst of all, they'll spit lies—they'll promise her the moon and all its stars, and then leave her in the dirt."

My mother slammed her teacup onto the table, cracking it—and making Claire and me jump in our chairs. She stared down at the broken cup in stifling silence, and I couldn't help wondering what exactly had happened to her that was so painful.

To be honest, I had no idea why my mother had brought Claire back with her. She always had an ulterior motive—usually to exact revenge, or to get her way. Now, hearing her speak of her painful past, and in a way that was clearly touching Claire's heart, a new theory wriggled itself into my head. Perhaps my mother had brought Claire to us to save her from experiencing all the terrible things my mother had gone through when she worked at a tavern. Perhaps she believed that, like her, Claire was destined to be much more than a tavern girl.

Could it be that Cora had finally done something out of the goodness of her heart? Something . . . *heroic?*

A knot formed in my throat as I pondered the possibility, and I quickly excused myself from the table before anyone noticed the tears welling up in my eyes.

February, six years earlier

I leaned back against the leather seat and closed my eyes as the carriage bumped and swerved along the snowy road. Mother and I had been to see a play at the royal castle. Now that I was ten years old, she wanted me to be "cultured," and even though I knew she only wanted the best for me, I'd struggled the whole while not to nod off. I'd focused on paying attention from when the velvety red curtain lifted to when it dropped, after the players had bowed and curtsied and the audience had clapped for what seemed like weeks. Culture might've been a good thing in Mother's book, but sometimes I wished she'd ask me what I wanted to do.

"It was a marvelous production," Mother said, patting my knee the same way she'd done dozens of times during the play.

"Yes," I murmured.

"I'm glad you enjoyed it. When you are queen, you'll be able to see that same play whenever you want. Or any you can imagine. You'll simply order it, and days later, it will come to life on stage, right before your eyes. When you are queen, you will have all the power in the land."

"Yes, Mother." I wrapped my cloak around my body, warding off the winter chill.

My mother called, "Hector! My daughter is cold," and the carriage came to an abrupt stop. A moment later, the coachman delivered two thick, furry blankets and then continued homebound.

Snuggled in the warmth of the blanket, I listened to the faint *clomp-clomp* of the horses and gazed out the window. Snowcapped trees lined the road, and every so often, I caught glimpses of deer and rabbits. Though I hadn't cared for the play, nor for meeting the other people who'd gone to see it, I rather enjoyed traveling to and from the castle in the snow-covered forest.

The carriage made a turn, and out my window, I saw ten or twelve children skating on a pond. They laughed and sang and made shapes on the snow-dusted ice. "Mother, look!" I said, pointing. She leaned over to see the children for herself. "That looks like so much fun. I want to join them," I said.

"We don't have your ice skates," she said.

I nodded sadly, squirming and twisting around to see the children for as long as possible from the carriage window. We kept rolling until she suddenly said, "Hector! Stop!"

Hector walked to her window, and she spoke with him in hushed tones. I waited patiently as the carriage turned around—a difficult and slightly scary task, as the road was icy—and headed back for the frozen pond. As soon as it stopped, Mother and I hopped out. I smiled up at her as she took my mittened hand. We plodded through the snow, over to the edge of the frozen pond.

"Little girl," my mother said, addressing a girl about my size. "My daughter wants to skate. Here is some money for your skates." She dropped some coins into the girl's hand. I grinned hopefully at the girl as she counted the coins, but then she handed them back to my mother.

"My father gave me these skates," she said. "They're not for sale." With that, the girl glided off and away, making figure eights with her friends in the middle of the pond. Clearly, the children were having a wonderful time. My heart swelled with the hope of not only getting to skate with them, but of becoming their friend.

I looked at my mother. "Try him," I suggested, pointing at a boy only slightly bigger than me. He was sitting on a log, whistling as he unlaced his skates. They weren't as nice or new as the girl's, but I did not care what condition they were in.

"My daughter wishes to join the girls," she told him. "I'd like to buy your skates." She showed the boy the money. He picked up one of the coins and bit it to make sure it was real. He thought about it for so long I truly believed he'd say yes, but he didn't. "It's not enough," he said, knotting his skates' laces together.

My mother's face turned red and she bit her lower lip. I was scared she was going to yell at him, or something much worse. But to my relief, she took a deep breath and grinned at him. "You're right. How foolish of me. *Your* skates are worth much more." She took a black velvet pouch from her pocket and poured every last coin into his palm. "There you go," she said. "What do you say?"

He studied the money and slowly stood. "My pa whipped me for coming home without my slingshot last Sunday. I hate to think what he'd do to me if I showed up without my skates."

"He'd be delighted his son knew a good deal when he saw it," my mother said, and I nodded encouragingly.

"I'm sorry, lady. Not today." After returning the money to her, he flung his skates over his back and walked away.

I was disappointed. The longer I'd stood there watching the children skating around and around the pond, the more I'd wanted to join them. If I'd had a pair of ice skates and a stranger offered me money for them, I couldn't say I would've sold them, either.

"It's all right, Mother," I said, tugging on her cloak. "Don't use magic. I can ice-skate another day." I actually liked that idea. "I'll bring my own and be really nice to the other children so they'll like me. Maybe I can become friends with them, and we can skate together regularly, like how Daddy goes hunting, or you play croquet."

"Why would you wish to be friends with such fools?" My mother's eyes flashed, and I knew something was about to happen. Something bad. I watched her out of the corner of my eye as we made our way across the snow to the carriage. Once we were inside, Hector closed the door. Wordlessly, my mother spread the blanket over my legs and stared straight ahead. I thought for a moment I had been wrong, and perhaps nothing bad was going to happen after all.

As I heard Hector crack the whip, a horrible shattering noise filled my ears. I peered out my window in time to see a huge ridge zigzag through the pond, splitting the ice into long, jagged pieces. The children's laughing and singing became screaming as they raced to the safety of the snowy bank.

The carriage sped off through the forest. I tried my hardest not to cry, but tears filled my eyes. I quickly wiped them away with the back of my mitten.

Fourteen

Saturday, May 20

The days leading up to the royal ball were joyous, and the jubilance of having won the Ogre Wars was decidedly contagious.

Normally, I would have been agitated when my mother forbade me from joining my father on his morning ride, saying she wanted me free of bruises and scrapes for the dance. But that day, I'd let it slide with little more than a sigh and devoted myself to a leisurely day indoors with my nose in a book and Thaddeus snoring at my feet.

The grandfather clock struck five, and I retired to my bedroom to begin getting ready for the evening. I took my time, brushing my hair until it shone and applying rouge to the apples of my cheeks. Next I selected one of my new gowns, a pale green one with white leaves embroidered on its bodice, matching slippers, and elbow-length gloves. Rainy styled my hair in a chignon accentuated with an emerald comb, and tendrils framed my face and neck. "You are a vision, m'lady," she said, and I hoped Jasper would think the same.

"Regina, it is time to go," called my mother from the landing. When I walked down the stairs, she whirled around in her form-fitting gray-and-gold gown and frowned at me. "Is that what you're wearing?"

"You bought it for me," I said, my good mood fading fast.

"Well, it simply won't do. Not for the royal ball. You're not a little girl anymore, Regina. With any luck, you'll meet your future husband tonight," she said. A small purple cloud formed in my mother's palm and then whisked over to fully envelop me.

Not a second later, I'd been magically dressed and

styled, from head to toe. My replacement gown was off-white silk, and when the light struck it, it seemed to flow down my body like cream into a bowl of berries. Its hem, sleeves, and neckline were trimmed in maroon lace. My hair was piled high in glossy ringlets, accented by a ruby-embellished headband. When I examined my reflection in the entryway mirror, I noticed my lips were painted, the beauty mark on the left side of my mouth was enhanced, and I'd been doused with more than a fair amount of rose water.

My overall appearance was overstated, I thought. Most of all, I was terribly uncomfortable. The corset nipped my waist until I could barely breathe, and my feet were stuffed into slippers two sizes too small.

"The shoes don't fit, Mother," I protested, lifting my gown to show her.

She arched an eyebrow. "The shoes are the perfect size," she said. "It's your feet that are too big."

I thought how wonderful it would be to have even the teensiest bit of magic, like Claire or the blind witch, so I could switch my shoes for ones more comfortable. I opened my mouth to beg my mother for mercy, but then my father rounded the corner, decked out in a suit and cravat that coordinated with my mother's gown. Once he caught sight of me, his eyes twinkled like a thousand stars.

"Regina," he said simply. He held out his elbow and escorted me to the carriage.

When I smiled back at him, it was with my whole heart. He made me feel beautiful.

I stood at the top of the castle's grand staircase, tucked between my parents. Below, the light of the setting sun streamed through the magnificent three-story-high stained glass window, casting rainbows on the walls. Ball gowns of every design and color brought the dance floor below us alive, swirling and churning like waves in the sea. Eagerly, I scanned the room first for Claire, then for Jasper. Alas, I saw neither.

A short man in a white jacket and plumed cap stepped forward, and over the orchestral music, called, "Announcing Prince Henry and Princess Cora, and their beautiful daughter, Regina."

Heads turned and nodded in slow motion as we made our entrance into the grand ballroom. I glided my gloved fingers down the golden handrail, careful not to slip on the slick marble stairs. Once I reached the landing, I let out a relieved breath and hurried to catch up with my mother and father, who'd already queued up to greet our royal host and hostess.

The king's gray-streaked hair spilled out from under his immense gold crown, mixing seamlessly with the fur of his collar. He stood with his chest up and his toes pointed slightly out. The instant before my father had the chance to exchange pleasantries with him, a guard whispered something in the king's ear. With a grunt, the king excused himself and left his wife to greet us alone.

"I hope nothing is wrong," my father said after paying his respects to the queen.

Queen Eva wore a yellow gown that skimmed her

waist and spiraled to the floor, reminding me of the blind witch's meringue delight cookies. Her necklace fanned out over her chest in multiple strands of diamonds and emeralds, and her black tresses were piled high over her dainty diamond crown.

"I'm certain all is fine," Queen Eva said. "My guess is that he wants to practice his speech in front of the mirror before delivering it later this evening."

"I look forward to hearing him speak," my father said politely.

"As do we." My mother closed the space between herself and our hostess.

"Cora. It has been a long while," Queen Eva said flatly.

"Indeed, it has," my mother said. "How is the lovely Snow White?"

"She is well," Eva said, grinning just enough to bring out a youthful-looking dimple. "She's a vivacious girl, the apple of her father's eye. He lives to make her happy."

"How nice. Clearly, Leopold has made *you* happy, as well."

I held my breath, hoping my mother would continue behaving cordially.

Eva's pale blue eyes flitted around the grandeur that surrounded us. "I cannot complain. It is a good life."

"Yes, it must be," my mother said, stepping forward to scrutinize Eva's face. "I can tell you smile quite often. The lines around your eyes and mouth do not lie."

The queen's eyes darkened, but to her credit, she showed no other signs of bristling at my mother's barbed comment. Instead, she looked beyond my mother and flashed me a tempered smile. "Regina, you've become a lovely young woman," she said, not unkindly.

"Thank you, Your Majesty," I said.

"I know a man who'll be especially delighted to learn you're in his presence."

Who? I wondered. *Could it be Jasper?*

"Oh, really?" my mother asked. "One of your guests has an interest in making my daughter's acquaintance?"

My heart skipped a few beats. I silently begged the queen not to name Jasper. If my mother knew I'd arranged a secret meeting with my art teacher, I didn't even want to think about what would happen to him, or to me.

"Benjamin is his name," Eva said offhandedly as she received the bluish-haired woman who'd been waiting behind us. I was so relieved Eva hadn't said Jasper's name, I almost twirled in circles.

"And he is a . . . ?" my mother prompted, blocking the older woman from entering the ballroom.

"Close personal friend of mine. He's staying with us here at the castle for several weeks." Though she was responding to my mother, the queen fixed her gaze on me, adding, "And he's a prince."

Fifteen

The aromas of the food made my mouth water, and while my father and mother began circulating, no doubt hunting down the prince Queen Eva had mentioned, I slipped into the banquet hall. The tables were draped in fine white linen, adorned with ornate floral arrangements, garlands, and candelabra. A trio of ladies dressed in white aprons bustled between the kitchen and the impossibly long tables, making sure the silver serving dishes were laden with fruit, vegetables, and roasted meats, and the baskets bursting with an assortment of freshly baked breads. I placed a small baguette on my plate, followed by some grapes and berries. It was when I approached the roasted lamb that I accidentally bumped into a man.

"Oh, pardon me," I said, scarcely glancing at him. "I must have been under the spell of the rack of lamb. It makes one abnormally clumsy, I hear."

"Then I must be under the same spell every day," he said, and though I'd already shuffled over to the dessert table, I could feel his eyes on me. A moment later, he materialized beside the colossal chocolate cake.

"You must be Regina," the man said, tilting his head upward. The top of his head rose only to my nose. He looked to be about three times my age, with a floppy reddish mustache, a scraggly beard that seemed to be holding on to the point of his chin for dear life, and baggy folds of skin under his eyes that reminded me of Thaddeus's. He dressed like a gentleman of means, complete with a ruffled cravat, a royal-blue jacket tailored to his barrel-shaped chest, and gleaming pointy-toed shoes. Yet he smelled like he'd taken a roll in a cabbage patch. I tried not to scrunch my nose and hoped the stench wouldn't make me lose my appetite.

"Yes, I am," I said. I knew I should ask him to introduce himself and engage in polite small talk as I drizzled sweet cream on top of a slice of cherry pie. But since no one other than the servants was around to witness my less-than-cordial behavior, I opted not to. Besides, I didn't want to encourage him, as I knew my mother would track me down with the prince in tow any moment. I needed to hurry and eat before I'd be stuck dancing with him—or any other noblemen or royals turned up by my mother's inexhaustible matchmaking efforts.

"Do you need any help carrying your plate?" he asked. He already had a large plate, a smaller one, and a cup in his hands, which made me curious as to how he planned to accomplish his proposed feat.

"If you're a juggler, I'm afraid you have the costume all wrong," I said.

He narrowed his eyes as if trying to interpret what I'd said. Realizing he wasn't going to leave me alone, I sighed and faced him. "I can manage fine by myself, thank you."

Luckily, Claire appeared in the banquet hall and

came straight over. She wore an elegant rose-colored gown that matched her lips, and her hair looped around in a multitude of twists and braids. "Pardon me," she said to the man, giving him a little curtsy before sweeping me away by my elbow. "I thought I might find you in here," she said, drawing me into a warm embrace. "Have you ever seen such an exquisite castle? So many beautiful people, all in one place? And this feast! It's enough to feed the entire kingdom." She was grinning from ear to ear and practically hopping up and down. I smiled at my friend, realizing I'd felt just as giddy when I'd gone to my first ball two years earlier.

I'd hoped the man would finally see himself away from me, but he was suddenly right beside us. "Hello," Claire said to him. "My name is Claire Fairchild. And you're . . . ?"

"Benjamin," he said as he gave his britches a hitch.

"The prince?" I asked, hoping against all hope there were two men at the ball called Benjamin, and that this one was not the prince Queen Eva had told my mother about.

"Yes," he confirmed. "I've been wanting to make your acquaintance for quite some time, Regina."

"Oh," was all I could say as I tried to suppress my instinct to run away as fast as possible in my ill-fitting shoes. Perhaps my mother wouldn't find him after all, and instead she would discover someone closer to my own age and my own height, or who at the very least didn't smell like a vegetable. Now that I knew who he was, I could at least do everything in my power to interfere with my mother's finding him—and I was sure Claire would help, too.

However, my scheming was in vain, because just then my parents appeared at the entrance to the banquet room, and my mother pinned me with her gaze. My father made a beeline for the baskets of bread, which came as no surprise. Meanwhile, my mother called, "Prince Benjamin," and sidled up to him as if they were old friends. "I see you've met my beautiful daughter, Regina. Isn't she a vision?"

"She is," Benjamin agreed, setting his drink on the edge of a table.

I exchanged a look with Claire, and while I was sure my eyes were riddled with desperation, hers twinkled with laughter. My mother grabbed hold of my shoulder and brought me back into her conversation.

"Well, maybe you should ask her to dance," my mother said, brushing a stray curl off my face as she spoke to the older man. "That is, if you're not already betrothed."

Seeing as how her old nemesis was the one who'd mentioned him, I didn't blame her for being extra cautious. I *did* blame her, however, for continuing the discussion when she could plainly see how undesirable he was.

"I'm as free as a stag," he said, taking a rather large bite of meat. "But I'm not surprised you thought as such. Gentlemen such as myself rarely wait as long as I have after the death of their wives before wedding another," he mumbled as he chewed.

"I'm sorry to hear your wife passed," my mother said, pulling a long face. "How long ago, may I ask?"

"Just shy of two and a half years."

"Goodness, Benjamin. Forgive me for being blunt, but it seems to me you simply haven't found the right lady to become your second wife."

"Third," he corrected her. "I've already had two. The first one perished in the Ogre Wars. The second just off and disappeared, without a trace." Oh, how I wished *I* could disappear right then. "It was a blustery winter solstice, and she'd gone out with her friends. Only none of her friends ever saw her that night. One can only conclude she is no longer alive."

"Yes, that would be the logical explanation," my mother said. "I'm so sorry for your losses."

"As am I," I added, a little bit late.

He shrugged and, to my relief, used a napkin to dislodge the bits of food from his mustache. He grinned at me, his yellowish teeth gleaming. "Yes, I believe you're correct. I need to meet the right lady. And I pray I do, for as you can see, I am not getting any younger."

A snort escaped Claire, and I elbowed her behind

Benjamin's back to make her stop. Thankfully, the man was so immersed in his monologue he didn't seem to notice, and Claire took my hint and disappeared.

"Then again, I *am* getting wealthier, and that is nothing to pooh-pooh," he added, fingering the gaudy gold pendant that hung from his neck.

Almost as if by magic—or perhaps it *was* magic—the orchestra began a cheerful little waltz. "Regina likes to waltz," my mother said, filling me with dread as a servant filled her cup with wine.

Benjamin sniffed, which made his mustache flutter in a most peculiar way. "May I have this dance, Regina?"

My mother beamed triumphantly at me as she took my plate and set it on the servant's tray. The aproned woman whisked away my untouched food, and I wished I'd taken at least a bite of it, especially the cherry pie. At least then I would've had something nice in my belly and sweet in my memory to carry me through what was destined to be a loathsome dance.

I raised my eyes to my father, but he was queued up

for a slice of mutton and probably had no idea what his daughter was being forced to do. Sadly, I didn't think he would have rescued me, anyhow. One dance with the old widower wouldn't kill me, I told myself. Unless I considered my slippers. I didn't know how much longer my feet could stand being so severely squashed.

I had no choice but to take Benjamin's proffered hand, which felt moist, even through my glove. He pulled a strange face, like a baby bird wanting to be fed, but with his head bowed down. At first I thought he might be choking, or even having a heart attack. And I admit a small part of me hoped the prince was suffering from some sort of medical condition. Nothing too deadly, but an ailment serious enough to keep me from having to dance with him.

When it dawned on me that Benjamin's birdie act was actually an awkward attempt at kissing my hand, I didn't know whether to pity him or myself. I decided to make it easy for him, and placed my hand beneath his puckered lips. My mother looked on with a spark of approval in her eyes as I ventured out into the ballroom at Benjamin's side. When I turned to look at her once more, I saw my father ask her to dance, but she just shook her head and walked away.

It might have been my imagination, but when Benjamin led me onto the floor, it seemed as though the dancing couples parted like a giant colorful curtain, turning their heads and training their gazes on our every move. Although I felt my heart sink, I held my carriage straight and proper as my partner whispered, "One, two, threeeee; one, two, threeee," loud enough for not only me, but anyone waltzing around us, to hear. I tried to think about something positive, such as meeting Jasper at the bridge later that evening. However, I hadn't seen my art teacher, and I was beginning to wonder if he'd come to the castle at all.

The prince left much to be desired as far as dance partners went, what with his limp arms, his pathetic sense of rhythm, and his uncanny knack for stepping on my already throbbing toes. Behind my smile, I was silently cursing Benjamin. And when I ran out of curses for him, I began afresh, cursing my mother and Queen Eva in turn. Just when I thought the song would never end, the musicians finally showed mercy.

I curtsied and thanked Benjamin, already searching the crowd for Claire as I backed away from my dance partner. Where could she be? I wondered. The orchestra began a new song, and before I could slip away, the prince asked, "Would you do me the honor of another dance, Regina?"

"That's very kind of you. However, I'm afraid my feet are beginning to ache," I said, hoping that would be the end of it.

"I understand," he said, and for some silly reason, I actually believed him. I began walking off the dance floor, still searching for my friend, when I noticed he was walking in step with me. "We don't have to dance. We don't have to stand at all. I know of a bench in the courtyard. It's off the beaten path, so to speak, and we can sit under the moon and stars, and get to know one another better." The thought of being alone with Benjamin made my stomach turn, and the way he raised his bushy brows sent a wave of nausea through it.

"I've been entertaining the notion of courting you," he continued, puffing out his chest. "The two of us make a fine couple. And, as your mother so sensibly stated, up until now, I've not found the right lady to become my third wife." I tried to turn my head before he saw that my eyes were bugging out, but he did notice—and grossly misinterpret—my response, because he quickly added, "But do not worry, Regina. Third and *final* wife. After all, you are younger than I, and you seem to be healthy. Therefore, I would wager you will be alive and well till the end of my years, and will have the great honor of tending to me until then." As he chuckled and hitched up his pants, I once again felt the urge to run away. But out of the corner of my eye, I caught a glimpse of a familiar rose-colored gown.

"There you are," Claire said, clasping her hands behind her back and rocking on her feet. "I realize this is most unconventional, but I was hoping I could have this dance."

Benjamin's ruddy face lit up. "Why, of course," he answered, giving the tip of his nose a quick dab with his handkerchief.

Unlike the prince, I wasn't sure what to think of my friend's boldness. Then again, cutting in on our dance was definitely less dramatic—and safer—than setting his shoes on fire.

"Thank you. Despite what the others say, you truly are a gentleman." And with that, Claire surprised both Benjamin and me by taking *my* hands. She twirled me around the dance floor, paying no mind to the direction in which the other dancers were moving. We narrowly missed colliding with several couples. But it was the prince's face—contorted in a way that made him look like a jester—that made us start laughing uncontrollably. I knew we had to get off the dance floor and out of the ballroom before anyone caught on to what had just happened.

Claire must have had the same thought, because she dragged me away, through the banquet hall, down a small corridor, and finally into the sweltering, smoky kitchen. A trio of cooks worked tirelessly, baking, roasting, and washing dishes. They only acknowledged us with slight nods as we zipped through into a windowless room in the back corner.

"What are we doing in the pantry?" I asked. It was a sizable space, double the dimensions of ours back home. The wooden shelves were stacked with produce, bags, and jars. I had no doubt King Leopold and Queen Eva's pantry stored enough ingredients and supplies to feed a multitude of families for weeks on end. I shrank away from a ghastly spiderweb draped between the broomstick and a crate, praying its spinner wasn't home. Still, it was a private nook, at least for the time being, and there was something exciting and yet cozy about hiding in there with Claire. I slipped off my shoes and gloves and tossed them on the floor. I'd been laughing so hard my stomach ached and I felt breathless and lightheaded. It was wonderful.

"You'll see." Claire winked at me and then stood up on her tiptoes and reached high—over the shelves stacked with produce, baskets, and sacks. From the very top shelf, she brought down a large jar full of golden-brown liquid.

"What is that?" I asked.

Her rosy lips curved into a smirk, and her eyes glittered in the low light. "Cider."

"How did you know it was up there?"

She shrugged. "Isn't that where the good stuff is always kept?" She unscrewed the lid and held out the jar for me to take a swig. First I took a sniff. It smelled of apples, perhaps on the rotten side, and vinegar—a sweet, slightly spicy aroma that was not altogether repugnant.

"Oh, yes. Of course," I said, pretending to be in the know. I had never tried cider before, so I wasn't sure what to expect. I surely didn't expect it to taste quite that good on my tongue or to burn so tantalizingly when it slid down my throat. It felt like slipping slowly into a steaming bath.

"What do you think?" Claire asked, watching me closely.

To be sure, I took another sip before handing it back to her. "It's delicious," I said, wiping my lips with the back of my hand. We passed the jug back and forth, each taking one more pull than our previous turn. At some point, we slid down the walls and rested our bottoms on the floor, despite its questionable cleanliness and our cumbersome, expensive gowns. I landed on one of my shoes, yanked it out from under me, and tossed it aside. We launched a whole new round of giggles when it landed on a pile of potatoes. Then Claire let out a very unladylike belch, and we were beside ourselves.

"Claire, you're my hero. I cannot thank you enough for saving me from having to suffer through another dance with that man. My mother wants me to be queen someday and feels like the more royals I meet, the better my chances."

"It was my pleasure," she said.

"I have to confess, you had me going for a moment. I thought you actually wanted to dance with him."

"Regina, really?" She patted down a pouf in her gown,

and it rebelliously sprang back up. "You know me better than that. Why, I'd rather dance with the crazy carpenter, Geppetto, than that old, sniveling, pitiful excuse for a prince." She thrust her fist into the skirt of her gown, and finally it stayed down.

I'd never heard of Geppetto, but if he was indeed crazy, I didn't feel left out. I knew enough loonies, thank you very much. I took another drink of the cider and handed it back to my friend, who knocked some back without hesitation.

I didn't know why—maybe Claire's mention of marriage—but suddenly I felt a zap of panic. "My mother cannot find out what we are doing," I said, nudging the door closed with my stockinged foot. "She'll be greatly disappointed if she finds out we gave the prince the slip. She's probably looking for me, and . . ." My heart raced at the thought.

Claire leaned forward and briefly pressed her finger on my lips. "It will be all right," she said. "She won't find out." She handed me the jar.

"She won't?"

Claire shook her head side to side. Her braids had begun to unfurl into long wavy tresses. She resembled a mermaid from my childhood storybooks.

"I don't want to frighten you, but I don't think you realize how very powerful my mother is," I said. "If she doesn't get what she wants, she can do terrible things."

A terror-stricken look flashed across Claire's face, as if something evil were breathing down my neck and she were powerless to stop it. But in the blink of an eye, it passed and was replaced by a languid smile. "I have no doubt she can," she said. "But Cora would never hurt you, Regina. I mean, *really* hurt you. You know that, don't you?" Sandwiching my hands in hers, she tilted her head as she waited for my answer.

"I guess so."

She dropped my hands and snatched the cider from me. "Good." She took a long draw, opening her throat to the warm, sweet liquid. "All right, let's go." She scooped up our shoes and tossed mine at me. I only caught one and had to poke my head between two bags of flour to find the other. My hands fumbled, and I almost lost my balance. I never believed myself to be overly graceful, but it seemed my brain was taking an unusually long while to function. Everything seemed fuzzy somehow. "Where are we off to now?" I asked.

"To explore the castle, of course."

Sixteen

As Claire and I slunk past the ballroom, I held my breath, praying my mother wouldn't spy us. "Look who it is," Claire said, pointing out the loathsome Benjamin, who was leaning against a wall. Next to him stood a woman barely wider than a broomstick, with a most unfortunate shade of orange hair. Though it appeared she was trying to chat him up, he was staring at the dancers with bleary eyes, erratically moving up and down to the music.

"He looks like a bear scratching its back against a tree trunk," I said, and Claire yanked me around to the backside of a pillar and stifled her giggles to keep him from noticing us.

The song came to an end, and the dancers escorted their partners off the dance floor. A hush fell upon the ballroom. King Leopold stood before the great battlefield mural, pacing to and fro as his booming voice filled the enormous room. "Thanks to the undeniable prowess and power of the royal army, and the courage and faith of the people at large, I am pleased to announce our kingdom is safe from the tyranny of the ogres, once and for all." The king twirled the tip of his mustache while the crowd burst into applause. He waited for complete silence and then cleared his throat before continuing. "Although our victory is sweet, it has come with a steep price. In the darkest of times, the ogres have slain our loved ones, burnt our villages to the ground, and pillaged crops, livestock, and precious heirlooms.

"But, knowing they have been bested, the surviving beasts have indeed surrendered. They have retreated into the outlying regions of the Enchanted Forest, where they shall lick their wounds and leave us in peace. We have stepped out of the debris, my loyal subjects, leaving behind our darkest days, and have marched into the light with our heads held high and our hearts full. We are victorious!"

Again, the guests clapped and cheered. Claire and I took advantage of the ensuing commotion to snake through the back row of people, hopefully unnoticed. That's when I caught a glimpse of my mother's gray-and-gold gown. She and my father stood at the front of the ballroom, appearing to be quite at ease in the company of the kingdom's most elite and celebrated.

We ducked into a hall accented with a tall arched ceiling, and it opened into a formal dining hall with a life-sized portrait of Queen Eva holding a cherubic little girl, who must have been Princess Snow White. They wore matching yellow dresses with royal-blue sashes, and the bottom right corner of the painting bore the signature of Jasper Holding.

"Is it ten o'clock yet?" I wondered aloud.

"Is that when you're cursed to turn into a mouse?" Claire joked, and then her memory must have clicked.

"That's right, your scandalous appointment with your art teacher." She clapped her hand over her mouth and giggled.

"I don't think Jasper is here at the castle. At least, I haven't spotted him. Have you, by chance?" I asked.

Claire shook her head. "I haven't. Perhaps he looks so different when he's all spiffed up that neither of us have recognized him. Or maybe he's on the periphery of the festivities, waiting patiently to meet up with you."

I grinned at the notion, thankful she was finally allowing me to indulge in my romantic whimsies, even if we were grasping at straws. Then again, it wasn't that long ago people thought it impossible to turn straw into gold, I mused with a spark of hope.

A couple strolled by in their finery. Claire gave them a funny curled-finger wave, covering her mouth and laughing when a hiccup escaped. Before gliding silently onward, the duo made it a point to peer down their noses at us. I shrugged them off and turned to look at the painting again.

There was something different about the way Jasper had painted Eva and Snow White from the way he'd more recently painted my parents and me. Certainly, he'd had some more experience by the time my mother had commissioned him, but it wasn't the quality of the work that stood out for me. I couldn't put my finger on it, but there was something in the way the light reflected in Eva's and her daughter's eyes. Something that at once made me smile to myself and caused the pit of my stomach to burn with jealousy.

"Guard!" Claire said, grabbing my hand and dragging me behind her. At first I figured she was merely playing some silly drunken game. But then I saw a pair of guards, dressed entirely in dark gray, with the king's emblem marking their breastplates. Their boots clanked as they marched across the marble floor, echoing loudly and ominously up and down the walls.

"You there, halt!" one of the guards called in a gruff voice.

Still holding my hand, Claire began running. Up

ahead, the hall forked. Another guard stood in the hallway to the left, but by the way he leaned against a cabinet, it appeared he'd dozed off. The hall on the right appeared to be clear, however, so that was the way we ran. We skirted a corner, sliding on the slick floor, only to find ourselves eye-to-neck with a giant stuffed bear, which was reared up on its hind legs. With its paws outstretched, its massive head tilted to the side, and its jaw open, showing off a mouthful of glinting teeth, it looked as if it had been frozen in time a split second before it had the chance to kill something—or someone.

Soon we would be surrounded by guards: a new one made his way toward us from in front, and the two behind us would certainly catch up. Any second, all three of them would catch sight of us and, at best, escort us back to the ballroom; at worst, I couldn't stand to imagine. Heart thudding, I grabbed Claire's wrist and pulled her behind the enormous beast. As the guards' footfalls clanked faster and closer still, we sank into its thick, dark brown fur and held our breath.

Two of the guards hustled past, but one paused right in front of the bear. We heard the squeak of the third man's armor as he turned his head side to side. Finally, he cursed under his breath and started marching down the hall. I exhaled the breath I'd been holding, and suddenly his footsteps stopped again. Claire squeezed my arm and I clenched my eyes shut. The guard started coming back in our direction. Had he heard me? Had he spied swaths of cream- and rose-colored fabric peeking out from between the bear's legs?

Miraculously, he strode straight past us, without so much as a pause in front of our furry, ferocious cover. As soon as we thought the coast was clear, we came out from behind the bear and scurried in the direction of the ballroom. But no sooner had we rounded the bend than we heard the clanking of guards' footfalls and a man's voice saying, "They went this way." Any second, they'd be face to face with us! We could run down the hall from which we'd just come, or we could try to give them the slip once more.

I spotted a doorknob by Claire's elbow and reached out to twist it. The door creaked ajar, and though we had no idea where it led, we ducked inside. We closed the door and braced our backs against it, collectively holding our breath as we heard the guards' boots pound by. It seemed the guards hadn't noticed our disappearing act, thank goodness.

Once my vision adjusted to the dim lighting, I saw before me a sizable chamber aglow with numerous sconces and candles. A canopy bed sat prettily in the middle, its posts and headboard carved with leaves, blossoms, deer, and an occasional bird. Barely above the sound of my heartbeat, I heard a melody so sweet and inviting, it sounded as if it were being played by a fairy on a miniature harp.

Claire elbowed me and pointed over to the window bay, where a woman slouched on a plush high-backed chair. Her large shoeless feet rested on a fringed stool. I braced myself for her to awaken and catch us where we shouldn't be. When a soft snore eased out of the woman's open mouth, I finally allowed myself to breathe; that's when the strong perfume of fresh roses filled my nostrils.

Indeed, fresh flowers covered every table and bureau, along with lovely dolls and ornate music boxes. One of the larger music boxes was open, revealing a fairy figurine that twirled in time to the music amidst an enviable assortment of jewelry. Claire obviously noticed it, as well, because she stepped toward it.

The music box eked out a last measure or two before going silent. Out of the corner of my eye, I saw something move. Whatever it was, it was careening straight for my friend! I grabbed the closest thing within reach—which happened to be a candleholder the size of my arm—and swung at it. I connected with something hard, and it clanked like metal. Gripping the candleholder, I positioned myself to strike a second time.

From the shadows came a hushed, "Oh, no!"

As Claire and I slid behind an armoire, I caught my first glimpse of the attacker as she bolted across the floor. With her dark hair and billowing nightgown, there was no mistaking her for anyone besides Princess Snow White. She landed in bed as smoothly as if she'd been diving into a lake. Claire—who'd stopped in her tracks—and I exchanged a look. With her wide-open eyes and gaping mouth, my friend appeared to be as confused as I was about the little girl's behavior. And yet, for some strange reason I could not say, neither of us made a move to escape. Instead, we simply slipped behind a massive chest of drawers.

"What—what was that?" the woman by the window asked in an alarmed yet groggy voice. "Snow, are you quite all right?" She stumbled over to the foot of the young princess's bed.

After the princess laid a candleholder—evidently the one she'd tried to club Claire with—on the rug beside her bed, she briefly faced our way and pressed her finger to her lips. "It is nothing, dear Johanna. I merely knocked over my candelabrum again."

"Gracious, my darling girl," Johanna said with a light chuckle. Clearly, she had no idea two intruders were in the room. That must have been how Snow White wanted it, or else she would have alerted the woman. "With all that tossing and turning you do in bed, my heart goes out to the poor wretch who'll end up married to you."

Snow White harrumphed and crossed her arms over her chest. "If I've told you once, I've told you a thousand times. I do not wish to be married, *ever*. So you needn't worry about any poor wretch."

Johanna chuckled again. "Well, *that*'s a relief," she said. I peeked out just in time to see her finish putting on her shoes. Next she began shuffling across the princess's bedroom. Any second, she'd surely spot Claire and me and call the guards to take us away.

I held my breath and felt Claire's muscles tense.

"Talking of 'relief,' I need to excuse myself for a moment," Johanna said, opening the door. "Meanwhile, get your beauty sleep—although you're already as fair as they come." With that, the woman ambled into the hallway, closing the door behind her.

Claire and I exhaled in unison.

"You two can come out now," Snow said. She angled her entire body toward us, dangling her legs over the edge of her oversized bed, and fixed us with a fierce glare.

I was ready to make a run for it, so long as the hall was clear.

Claire had a different priority, though. After closing the distance between Snow and herself, she picked up the discarded candlestick. "What in the land? You tried to knock me on the head with this! You little—"

"Princess," Snow provided, holding up her chin. As the candlelight played on her features, I couldn't help noticing how truly beautiful she was. She had long black hair, lips as red as the apple I'd given Jasper, and creamy skin. Though her face hadn't lost the cherubic quality Jasper had captured in her portrait, she was already, at the mere age of seven or eight, a threat for eclipsing her mother's celebrated beauty. "I believe that is the word you were searching for."

Claire gnawed on her lower lip, and I could only

hope she was having second thoughts about pelting the girl with insults. After all, Snow *was* a princess. A beloved one, at that. She could tell her father to behead Claire, and in no time, a blond head with lifeless blue eyes would roll off the guillotine.

I hurried over to my friend and took her hand in mine, squeezing it in silent warning. "Yes, Your Highness," I said in a voice so syrupy it made my teeth ache. "You're wise to know that was what she meant to say."

Snow nodded once. "I thought as much." She slid her attention over to Claire and said, "The word I wanted to call *you* is *thief*. Because that is what you are—a dirty, rotten thief, sneaking into my chamber to steal my precious jewels."

Claire turned her head to look at the open music box on the bureau, which only made her look guiltier. My heart pounded, and I realized we were not out of the woods yet. Any minute, Claire and I could be at the mercy of King Leopold and Queen Eva—unless we could smooth things over with their daughter. "I realize it looks like we were trying to rob you," I said, "but we can explain—"

"*She* is a thief; however, *you*'re something worse," she interrupted, her big brown eyes boring into me.

Now the girl was getting on my last nerve, princess or not. I gritted my teeth, forcing myself to rein in my anger. Against my better judgment, I asked, "And what is that, pray tell?"

"You are a tagalong. You're too scared to do the dirty work yourself." When neither Claire nor I replied, she added, "You're always behind someone else, hiding in shadows. You never know what you are missing." Seemingly pleased with herself, Snow smoothed her dark tresses over her shoulder.

I mulled over Snow's words for a brief moment, and when I failed to find any real meaning, I dismissed them as rubbish. She was only a child. She'd likely heard the same words delivered by a marionette in a puppet show or one of those women in black dresses and head scarves who loitered in alleys. Besides, her nanny would surely be returning any second, and Claire and I needed to get out of there and back to the ball.

Claire spoke up. "With all due respect, Your Highness, my friend is not a tagalong. You'll be glad to hear she's inclined to get into all sorts of trouble." After giving my hand a quick squeeze, she dropped it and crossed her arms, daring the girl to believe it. "In fact, at the ten o'clock hour, I wouldn't be surprised if she got herself into trouble right here, at your castle."

Snow's eyes glinted, and her youth revealed itself when she bounced on the mattress in evident eagerness. "Really?" she said. "I'd love to hear the stories!"

Suddenly, I saw Snow in a new light. Yes, she was born of the wealthiest, most powerful royal family in the entire Enchanted Forest. Yes, she was fair beyond comparison. And yet, under all of that pomp was a lonely little girl. Someone who reminded me of myself before Claire had become my friend.

Maybe the cider was to blame, but I felt a warm surge of gratefulness for Claire.

"It's getting late, Your Highness," Claire said, glancing at the beautiful clock on Snow's bedside table. "Your nanny will be back anytime now. We must be going."

"Oh, no! Johanna will be gone quite a while longer. Trust me, she is not quick about her business," Snow White said. "Please stay a little while longer."

"How about we make it a bedtime story, Princess?" Claire suggested.

"How about you call me Snow? Now, what shall I call the two of you, unless you'd like me to call you Thief and Tagalong?"

I laughed, my heart softening even more for Snow. "I think Thief and Tagalong will do." I slid my gaze over to watch Claire's reaction to my answer. When she beamed at me, I exhaled in relief. I didn't want to tell Snow my real name for fear she'd know there was bad blood between our families.

Snow patted the mattress beside her. Claire and I hesitated, but she hit it even harder, insisting. "Don't worry. We've a good ten minutes before Johanna makes her way back to my chambers." After we sat, she put her warm little hand on mine and asked, "Will you tell me a bedtime story, Tagalong?"

The little girl's gentle touch and the way she implored me with her big brown eyes made my breath hitch. I couldn't put a finger on my sudden flood of emotions, nor whether the connection I felt was sisterly or maternal. All I knew was, it was too much.

"I've never told anyone a bedtime story," I said, hoping closing the topic would effectively stop all the sentimentality that was seeping into my heart.

Seventeen

I leaned against Snow White's pillows–which were even plumper than mine at home—and stared up at the ceiling. It had as many tiers as the most decadent wedding cake, rising upward beyond the lights' highest reaches, disappearing in blackness.

"Didn't your mother tell you stories when you couldn't fall asleep?" the princess asked.

"I must have never had trouble falling asleep," I said, though it wasn't true.

"Well, *I* did," Claire piped up. "My mother and I live above a tavern, and it's sometimes very loud."

"Just your mother and you?" Snow asked. "What happened to your father?"

"He left us when I was about your age," Claire said.

"Oh, I'm sorry," Snow said ever so softly. She placed her hand on Claire's.

"I'm not. He was a beast," Claire said. "We are better off without him, believe me."

My heart squeezed for Claire. "I never knew that."

"It's not something I like to talk about," she said.

"Haven't you any brothers or sisters?" Snow asked Claire. "I always wanted a big sister."

"I had a brother, once," Claire said. "Corbin was four years older than I, and he was brave and cunning. However, an ogre got the best of him. Three ogres, in fact. He perished in the war."

"No!" Snow said, her dark eyes round as the moon. "I am *so* sorry."

"Thank you," Claire said. "I like to think he died fighting to make the Enchanted Forest a better place for the rest of us."

"Oh, he did. He truly did," Snow said emphatically.

The three of us sat on the soft bed in reverence for quite a while before Snow broke the silence. "So, what story did your mother tell you when you couldn't sleep, Thief?"

"She told me a story about pirates," Claire said with a captivating hint of drama. "They'd scour the village, snatching up little children who were on the streets past their bedtime, tying them up and forcing them onto their ships."

"And then what?" Snow prompted.

"They'd sail far away, so far no one could hear the children scream as the pirates forced them to walk the plank."

"How awful!" Snow tapped her temple with her finger. "What if the children had started screaming straight-away, like the very moment they got on board? Then, if the pirates made them walk the plank anyway, they'd be close enough to the shoreline to swim home. They could run back to their homes and go to sleep. After they changed out of their wet clothes, of course."

"Oh, no," said Claire in a low voice. "The sea is teem-ing with deadly creatures, whether the waters are deep or shallow."

"Like what?" Snow asked, leaning forward.

"Crocodiles with teeth like butchers' knives. Giant octopuses that will wrap their tentacles around you . . ." she said, wrapping her arms around Snow. Snow let out a little scream and covered her mouth to keep more from coming out. Claire tightened her grasp and continued, "and crush the life out of you in two seconds flat. There are also mermaids with tails as sharp as daggers, and mouthfuls of teeth even sharper." Claire smiled at Snow and bared her teeth.

"I don't care for your story," Snow said, crossing her arms over her chest. "It's stupid. Mermaids don't hurt people. They just sing and brush their hair all the day long."

"Like Tagalong?" Claire said, laughing.

"I don't sing," I said. Now that I thought about it, I had probably been Snow's age the last time I'd sung. My parents had taken me to the springtime celebrations in the village, and the children were singing and dancing about a maypole with streamers of every color of the rainbow.

I was too shy at first, but with my father's gentle nudges, I eventually joined in. From the sidelines, he clapped and chuckled. My mother, however, crossed her arms over her chest, a frown darkening her face. Later, as we were in the carriage heading home, a wreath of fresh flowers crowning my head, she turned to me and said, "It's a good thing you're beautiful, my darling girl, because you are no nightingale." I swallowed the memory and turned back to the princess, who'd been watching me intently. "So, Snow," I said, afraid she was going to ask me yet again for a story. "If you're an expert on bedtime stories, let's hear one of yours."

"All right. Let's see." She pressed her finger under her chin as she thought. "I could tell you a story about the Blue Fairy. That's a wonderful tale Johanna loves to tell me. The Blue Fairy does so many nice things for people—all you have to do is go to Firefly Hill, find the blue star, and ask. As long as your heart is pure, she will grant your wish."

"Everyone's heard that story," I said, unimpressed.

Snow tapped under her chin. "Oh! I know another one. Now, this one is *really* scary, so be warned," she said melodramatically. "Deep in the darkest part of the forest, there lives a blind witch whose cottage is made entirely of gingerbread and other sweets. She lures children into her house and fattens them up. And then, *she eats them up for supper!*"

I couldn't believe my ears. "Yes, we've been there! We've met that witch. However, as you can plainly see, she did not eat us. Not even a nibble."

Snow scrunched her annoyingly perky nose. "You shouldn't fib to me. It's impolite."

"All right, have it your way, Princess. She *did* eat us," I jested.

"No! I mean, you shouldn't fib about having been at the gingerbread cottage," Snow said, rolling her eyes.

"Oh, but we *have*," Claire insisted. "The blind witch shared her cakes with us. Despite that, she wasn't exactly cordial. In fact, she blew us out of her cottage, which was a little extreme, if you ask me. And she stole my ring."

"Oh, no! Was it a special ring?" asked Snow.

Claire sighed. "Actually, yes. It was my brother Corbin's. The good vicar brought it to my ma before we buried him, and she gave it to me. It was gold with a cabochon garnet, and was carved in the shape of a dragon's claw. It was too large for my fingers, but I wore it around my neck on a chain." She paused and pressed her palm on her chest, over her heart. "It made me feel closer to him," she said in a sad, soft voice. I thought maybe she was going to cry, but when she looked over at us, she smiled. "I'm sure the blind witch doesn't really eat children. It must be a silly story adults tell to keep their own children from venturing too far into the woods."

Snow stared at Claire one moment, and me the next, like she couldn't quite wrap her mind around what we were telling her. "Pardon me for saying so, but you cannot know that for certain. You two are too *old* for her to eat. Your meat is tough and stringy and altogether unappetizing. She likes the tender meat of young children, such as myself." She held her head high, as if she took great pride in her tender meatiness.

"That may be, but I truly think you have nothing

to worry about. The witch probably made up the part about eating children herself," I said, "to keep pesky little youngsters from bothering her. That way, she can live in peace, eating all the sweets her heart desires and having her treasure all to herself."

"Treasure?" Claire said, smirking. "Nice touch. Oh, I know! We should go back to the gingerbread cottage and fill our pockets with the witch's booty."

"Don't invite the pirates," I said. "They'd keep it all for themselves. They can't really help themselves; it's what they do."

A huge grin spread over the young royal's face—broad enough that I spied a gap or two where her baby teeth had fallen out. "Ooooooh! What an adventure that would be! Will you take me with you? Of course, I would need a nickname, too. How about . . ."—she pressed her finger to her lips thoughtfully—"Bandit?" Claire and I exchanged a glance and tried to hold back our laughter. "I will be the one to find Corbin's dragon ring, because naturally the witch keeps it in the treasure room." The princess let out a big gaping yawn and promptly covered it with the back of her little hand. "I'm not afraid of that mean ol' witch. I'm not afraid of anybody, or anything." She barely eked out the last word before she yawned again.

Knowing it was time for us to leave, I leaned over and blew out her bedside candles. Snow let out a bloodcurdling scream, startling Claire and me right off the bed.

Johanna burst into the room. "Snow, darling, what is it? Why have your candles gone out?" She shot over to Snow's side like a cannonball. "Who is in here? You there, what do you want with the princess? Guard! Guard!"

"Johanna, please," Snow said calmly. "*Shhh.* Don't alert the guards. These are my friends. They've been keeping me company while you were gone. They came to the ball. See? Don't they look lovely? So lovely, in fact, *all* the gentlemen wanted to dance with them. They grew weary of dancing, and they've been telling me the most delightful bedtime stories ever since. Please, light my candles and I'll introduce you."

Although the woman watched us suspiciously, she did as Snow asked. Soon the royal chamber was once again bathed in a soft, flickering glow.

"I'm not proud of this," Snow said, turning her attention to Claire and me, "but I'm afraid of the dark."

"It's nothing to be ashamed of," I said. "I was afraid of the dark when I was your age, as well."

"Really?" she asked.

"Yes, really," I said, smiling.

"Well then, I guess there is hope for me yet." Snow went on to present the two of us to Johanna. "Johanna is my mother's personal maid, and she takes excellent care of me." The princess held her chin high and proud.

Johanna smoothed the fabric of her pinafore and shifted on her feet. "Except for tonight, it appears. I shouldn't have left you unsupervised."

"Don't fret one bit about it, Johanna. I promise I won't tell my parents. It will be our secret. Besides, I wasn't alone. My new best friends made sure of that." With another yawn, the princess wound a tiny music box on her bedside table, regaling us with its sweet, simple tune.

"This song reminds me of winter's first snowfall," she said, her words heavy with imminent slumber.

We bade good night to Snow and Johanna and returned to the ballroom. The music, dancing, eating, and drinking had continued despite our foray into the castle's restricted quarters. Not that I expected the gala to have come to a screeching halt in our absence, but I was more than a little surprised to see my mother milling about with a small highbrowed entourage as if she didn't even realize I wasn't behind her, waiting for her to fill my metaphorical dance card with eligible men.

For a split second, I thought she'd spotted me, and I held my breath. When her gaze continued its seamless rove over the crowd, I was convinced she had not. In her eyes, I was invisible; somehow, it didn't feel right.

In the distance, I heard a clock strike ten. "Oh, no. I should already be at the bridge." I silently cursed Snow for eating up so much of our time. "I'm going to be late."

"Maybe he's waiting for you," Claire said encouragingly. "Go. I'll keep an eye on Cora in case she asks about your whereabouts."

"Thank you, Claire."

"I'll be waiting right here for you." I turned to leave, but she grabbed my shoulder. "Regina? Promise me if he's not there, you won't be heartbroken."

"I promise," I said.

She smoothed my hair and gave my cheeks a pinch. "Promise if he *is* there, you won't forget about me."

"I'll never forget you, Claire Fairchild."

Eighteen

I trudged through the royal gardens by the glow of the moon, stars, and an occasional firefly, careful not to trip on the roots protruding from the pathway or, later, the jagged stepping stones. Once and again, I glanced over my shoulder, half expecting my mother to be storming after me.

I was so preoccupied with getting there in one piece that I arrived at the bridge before I'd had the opportunity to rehearse what to say to Jasper if indeed he was waiting for me. My nerves were frazzled. Even if I'd known what to say, it probably would have come out embarrassingly unintelligible.

Nevertheless, I needn't have worked myself up. He was not there.

As I stood looking at the bridge, an odd combination of disappointment and relief wrenched my stomach. The bridge had appeared so charming before, from the back of my horse. Its gentle slope and generous width offered an easy, dry passage from one side of the gurgling stream to the other. Its white paint was chipped here and there, and nearby bushes burst with dark pink roses like the ones that were in Snow's chamber. They flanked both banks, offering not only beauty but a sweet and rich fragrance.

But in the dark, it seemed like a sad and lonely place, leading nowhere new. Orchestral music wafted through the courtyard and into the gardens, heralding the resumption of the dancing in the ballroom.

A lump formed in my throat, and tears welled in my eyes. "You haven't the power to break my heart," I whispered to Jasper, wherever he might have been. For all I knew, he was watching me from somewhere in the gardens. Perhaps he'd been keeping an eye on me all night long. Grabbing the bottom of my gown, I rushed back toward the castle—and nearly ran into somebody as I rounded the fountain.

"Oh!" we said at the same time, and I gasped out loud when I realized it was Prince Benjamin.

"Regina. I was not expecting you," he said through his yellowish teeth as he grasped my shoulders to steady me. "I'm not disappointed to discover you've had a change of heart, though."

I wriggled out of his grasp. "I simply came outside to get some fresh air. I didn't realize anyone was out here. You haven't seen anyone else, perchance?"

He narrowed his eyes. "Are you looking for somebody in particular?"

"No," I said, probably too readily to have been believable. "I don't want to bump into anyone else out here. I'm, um . . . afraid of the dark," I said, borrowing Snow's line in a pathetic attempt to get away. "Now, if you'll kindly excuse me . . ." I stepped around him and resumed walking.

"Regina, wait!" Benjamin called after me. "I'll escort you back to the ballroom."

"There's really no need for that," I answered, hoping he would keep his distance. However, I heard his panting and heavy footfalls not far behind.

Thankfully, Claire was waiting to receive me at the door, and the instant I stepped in, she threaded her arm through mine. "It appears you have a new beau," she said, nodding at Benjamin, whose stubby legs had to work overtime to keep up with me.

"If I throw some salt on that slug, do you think he'll disappear?" I asked under my breath.

"There's only one way to find out," Claire said. "And I know where to find an entire block of it."

I loved how we didn't even have to talk about where we were really going or what we were going to do when we got there. By the time Benjamin arrived in the ballroom, we were gone. We veered off into the banquet hall and wended our way through the kitchen, where we had to sidestep a cook carrying a steaming pot and a greyhound snoozing beside the stove. Once we were back in the pantry, I shed my shoes and gloves, and Claire rose to the tips of her toes to reach the cider.

We settled into our previous positions, sitting on the floor and leaning against sacks of flour. I gladly accepted the jar she handed me.

"He wasn't there," I said flatly, staring down into the pungent amber-colored liquid.

Her eyes became glassy for a couple of seconds, and then she blinked. "I'm sorry, Regina." We each took a couple of swigs of cider before she said, "But I'm holding you to your promise. I won't allow you to be heartbroken."

I swallowed and forced a smile.

"I don't blame you if you want to leave," Claire said. "I'm sure my uncle won't mind taking us home."

Truth be told, I wasn't opposed to going to bed. If anything, my feet needed a break, and the thought of slipping under my covers sounded heavenly. "Too bad we can't return to Snow White's room, ask Johanna to tell us all a bedtime story, and fall asleep in that luxurious pink bed," I said in a joking tone, though I was only half jesting.

"Speaking of bedtime stories," Claire said, "did the blind witch really have a roomful of treasure?"

I nodded. "Yes. I don't know why I didn't mention it before. I just, well, kind of forgot about it until Snow had us telling her about it."

"Do you think what Snow said could be true?"

Snow White's voice sounded in my head. *You are a tagalong. Too scared to do the dirty work*. Her words were so clear it was as if she were sitting in the pantry with us. Perhaps it wasn't a bunch of childish drivel. Although our encounter had been brief, Snow saw something in me. Something I didn't much like, let alone care to admit. I didn't want to be a tagalong. I was tired of being a victim. I didn't want to live in fear. I wanted to come out from the shadows.

When I really thought about it, I wanted to be more like Claire. Only I wanted to be *me*. The real Regina. I wanted to rise up and show the world my mettle. That thought fired me up from the inside out.

"Regina?" Claire snapped her fingers in front of my face, jarring me out of my reverie. "Goodness! Have you had too much cider?"

"Probably," I said, and we both laughed.

"So, do you think Snow was right?" she asked once we settled down. She leaned against a bag of beans and rested her hands behind her head. It made her hair stick up like donkey ears.

"About my being a tagalong?"

She giggled again. "No! About the witch hoarding my brother's ring. I figured by now she'd likely have sold it to somebody, but if she does have a treasure room, do you think it's there?"

I shrugged. "It may be."

"I wish I could get it back." Her fingertips skimmed her collarbone.

The door suddenly swung open, narrowly missing my knees. A birdlike woman in an apron screeched at the sight of us and dropped the basket of fruit she'd been carrying. As Claire and I scrambled to our feet, another servant—this one twice the size of the first—came racing to the other's aid, and before we knew it, the pantry was populated with four fretful people, all talking at once.

Finally, I held up my hand in what I hoped was an authoritative way, and everybody quieted. "Excuse us," I said in a polite tone. "My friend and I were trying to show ourselves out, and we lost our way. Castles can be quite befuddling."

Nodding, Claire said, "This is my first time in a castle."

"It's true," I agreed, scrunching my feet into my slippers. "Can either of you please point us in the right direction? It's late, and her uncle's carriage is waiting."

The larger woman stooped, picked up the jar of cider, and gave it a good wiggle. "What, pray tell, is goin' on in here?" she demanded in a strange accent, eyeballing Claire and me.

I shrugged, and Claire pointed at the smaller woman. In turn, the smaller woman put her hands on her hips and huffed. While the two servants had words—as our ploy had obviously hit a nerve between them—Claire and I slipped behind them and out of the pantry. As we ran through the kitchen, I realized I'd left my gloves behind. I went back to retrieve them, only to see the smaller woman climb up the shelf and slap the other right on her cheek.

Somehow, Claire and I held in our fits of laughter until we collapsed in Giles's carriage. Before the coachman took off, however, there was a curt tapping on the window. I feared it was Benjamin and hoped it was Jasper.

It wasn't a man at all, though. Illuminated by fiery torches and colorful lanterns, my mother appeared every bit as put-together as when we'd first arrived at the ball. She curled her finger to say, *Come,* and I gathered my things and scooted across the bench.

Before stepping out, I gave Claire a look that I could only hope expressed what a wonderful night I'd had with her. She gave me a little wave and sank back into her seat, probably exhausted. I knew how she felt. But I also felt light—and a little tipsy—as I followed my mother down the hill.

"Did you have an enjoyable evening, my daughter?" she asked as we made our way down the hill past the carriages to where Hector was waiting with ours.

"Yes, Mother."

"Good. Your father will be joining us shortly. As we were leaving, Prince Benjamin asked to speak with him. It appears you made a good impression after all."

I stopped walking. "Does that make you happy?"

"Happy?" She chuckled softly. "Well, it's certainly something. Your first ball at sixteen, and already you've caught the eye of a man with royal blood." She reached over and brushed a piece of hair off my cheek.

With the colorful party lanterns flanking us and the moon and the stars shining from the sky, my mother was casting a very large shadow.

And I was in it.

Once I got home from the royal ball, I went directly to my chambers. I shed my shoes, gown, and corset, leaving them where they dropped. Then I sprawled out on top of my bedspread, replaying some of the scenes from the night. I had every intention of falling asleep just so, but someone rapped on my door.

"I've come for your laundry, m'lady," Rainy said, and I grunted something agreeable-sounding.

"Did you have a nice time at the ball?" she asked as she bustled about.

I rolled my eyes, wishing the woman would pick another time to be social.

"You looked very beautiful. I am sure the gents couldn't keep their eyes off you."

"The one I would have liked to have noticed me didn't even bother to show up, and the one who wouldn't leave me alone made me want to *throw up*."

"I'm sorry to hear it," she said, frowning. "I wager you had a lovely time with Miss Claire, though. You two have become fast friends, yes?"

"Yes, yes. A lovely time. Fast friends. Didn't you say you were coming for my laundry?"

Out of the corner of my eye, I spied her sniffing my

gown. When she regarded me, her eyes glossed with concern and her brow furrowed with what I interpreted to be disappointment. I could tell she believed I'd had too much drink and was feeling the ill effects.

In all honesty, my stomach *was* in a most fragile state. Whether from the cider or my emotions, I did not know. What I did know, however, was that I was sick and tired of being a "tagalong." I wanted to be courageous, like Claire. I wished to be powerful, like my mother. I was tired of letting fear rule my life.

I ungracefully slid off the bed and tromped to my vanity. Staring at my reflection, I wiped the streaks of makeup from my eyes. I shook my hair loose and gently touched the skin above my lip. I missed the girl who got back in the saddle the morning after her accident. I missed the girl who believed it was more important to win her own approval than her mother's. Maybe, possibly, if I could become that girl again, I would love the person in the mirror.

Before crawling into bed, I padded out onto my

balcony. The night sky was ablaze with stars. I sought out the brightest one, and it seemed to wink at me. Unlike the others, which shone like diamonds, this one was the color of a sapphire.

Nineteen

Sunday, May 21

The night after the royal ball, I grabbed a lantern and mounted my steed. I wasn't going to visit Claire as I'd told my parents. "To Firefly Hill," I said as I guided Rocinante southward, into the forest.

I had no idea if what I was about to do would work, or if it would be an utter waste of time. The tale of the Blue Fairy was as old as time, but as I was discovering, some of the stories I had been told or had read in books could very well be true, like that of the blind witch in the gingerbread cottage. I could only hope Firefly Hill was a real place, and that like in the story, it was located under the clearest part of the night sky. However, the farther I rode, the more disheartened I became, for each time I thought I might be in the right place, clouds rolled in. Rocinante seemed to feel my despair, and on several instances, he looked back in the direction of the stables.

I sighed. "All right, Rocinante. Let's go home." As soon as I'd said it, a firefly flew in front of us. Not a second later, it was joined by dozens, hundreds, maybe even thousands of others, all blinking their tiny yellow lights. They might as well have taken Rocinante's reins, because he sure-footedly followed their lead.

Before us, the hills, boulders, and trees of the Enchanted Forest sprawled as far as we could see, illuminated by the moonlight. "Oh, Rocinante, it's beautiful," I said breathlessly. The fireflies flew higher, leading our gazes upward. The canopy of leafy branches yawned open, revealing a velvety midnight-blue sky. "This must be the place."

Rocinante neighed and bobbed his head. I slid off the saddle and hitched him to a tree, leaning against its trunk while I scanned the stars for the blue one I'd seen before.

"It's hopeless," I complained to Rocinante after several moments had passed. My heart felt heavy as I searched the sea of stars in vain.

But as soon as I'd spoken, I caught a glimpse of a twinkling star, and the longer I stared at it, the bluer it became. "Maybe it's not hopeless after all," I murmured, mesmerized by the extra-bright flickers. I closed my eyes and made my wish.

Then I peeked—first with one eye, then the other. Nothing had changed. It was just me, my horse, and a bunch of fireflies on a hill. "Come on, Rocinante. This is a waste of time. The Blue Fairy doesn't really exist."

Rocinante pricked his ears and stomped his front leg. In the reflection of his eyes, I spotted a tiny blue dot. He kept his eyes trained on it as it floated around the tree-tops. By the time I whirled around to see it directly, the blue dot had drifted downward and grown to the size of an apple. It continued expanding as it hovered before me. A sudden flash of light blinded me momentarily, and I gasped and shielded my face.

When I lowered my hands and blinked, a resplendent fairy had appeared between Rocinante and me, gracefully flapping her translucent wings. Her gown reminded me of a summer sky—azure and airy—and was festooned with sweet-smelling roses. Her curly dark hair was piled on the top of her head, elegant and soft. She seemed to be sprinkled from head to toe with stardust.

"Hello," she said, smiling.

It took me a few seconds to find my voice. "Hello. Have you come to grant my wish?" I asked in shock. The Blue Fairy was floating before me, and what was more, we were actually communicating.

With lyrical grace, she at once tilted her head, blinked her eyes, and smiled. "Well, that depends on you. Please, tell me why you want it so badly."

I wandered over to my horse and slipped my fingers through his mane and down his neck. He pushed into my hand, wanting more. "When I was twelve, I went on a horseback ride with my father. The horse I was riding—this one's mother—got spooked when she lost sight of him, and bucked me into a tree. I fully believe she never meant me harm. Hwin was a wonderful horse, a true friend." *Was.* I swallowed, trying to keep the emotions I'd so carefully buried from coming back up. "The next day, when I was able to conquer my fear of getting back into the saddle, I felt courageous. At that moment, I liked myself—probably more than I ever have. I want to feel like that again."

"I see."

"So, are you able to grant my wish?"

She held up her dainty fingers, and in them appeared a gilded handheld mirror. "See for yourself."

As she passed me the mirror, a swarm of fireflies formed a wreath around it, lighting up my reflection. My gaze immediately gravitated to above the right corner of my mouth, where the cut I'd received when I'd fallen off Hwin had reappeared. The cut healed before my eyes, leaving behind a scar. I touched it, taken aback.

"It was there all along," the Blue Fairy said. "Your bravery. Now, if you ever question it, or need a reminder, you will be able to see it for yourself every time you look in the mirror."

As her words sank in, I couldn't help smiling. I examined the scar in the mirror, and the empowerment I'd felt four years before, when I'd gotten back on the horse, returned full force. "Not only have you granted my wish, you've reminded me what it feels like to have hope." If Snow White's and my path ever crossed again, I finally had a proper bedtime story to tell her.

I returned the mirror to its owner; however, in the instant our fingers brushed, the fairy gasped and jerked her hand away. It was as if my touch had somehow scorched her. The mirror fell on a moss-covered rock and shattered. "Oh, dear!" she exclaimed, and if I wasn't mistaken, it appeared she was trembling.

"Is something wrong?"

"To be honest, I'm not sure. Your heart is pure. If it were not, I wouldn't have been able to grant your wish."

She hung in the air, perfectly motionless. Slowly, she bent her elbows and flipped her hands palms up. "You see, fairy magic is the purest of all light magic. Yet, when I touched you, I sensed something. . . ." Her hands squeezed into fists, and she dropped them to her sides.

"What did you sense?" I prompted, though I wasn't sure I wanted to hear the answer. *Is there something wrong with me?*

She swallowed and smiled, but the smile didn't reach her eyes. "Oh, never mind, child. I'm sure it meant nothing. Absolutely nothing. Nothing . . . at all."

I'd only just met the Blue Fairy, but I could tell she was lying. "Something is troubling you. Please, tell me what it is," I beseeched her.

A look of alarm flashed over her features.

"What did you sense?" I repeated.

Her shoulders slumped, which made her wings appear flimsy and sad. "Promise me you will never forget this moment, when your heart was so pure, I had no choice but to grant your wish—and do so without reservation."

She turned her eyes skyward for a brief moment and then stretched out her wings. "Always remember the way it feels in the core of your heart, and in the depths of your soul," she said as she took to the air. "Come back to this moment whenever you're torn between light and dark. Promise me."

Torn between light and *dark?* "I promise," I agreed. But I was certain I'd never have reason to revisit this moment again. I wouldn't be drawn to . . . darkness.

I mounted Rocinante and he turned on his hind legs, waving his majestic tail behind him. I searched the night sky for the Blue Fairy to thank her, but she was nowhere to be seen. I raised my gaze higher, and the blue star twinkled brightly for a mere second before dimming to blend in among the sea of stars.

"Your Highness, Regina is home," Solomon announced, discreetly yawning as he scratched his belly.

"Thank you, Solomon." My mother entered the living

room in a cloud of the latest perfume she'd talked my father into procuring for her. She wore a deep-blue gown trimmed with black, accessorized with gold and sapphire jewelry. She placed a vaseful of orchids on the sofa table and took extra care and time to straighten them to her liking. Evidently, they were not her choice color, and so she waved her hand and they deepened in hue from a blush pink to a deeper mauve, and finally, to a dramatic shade of crimson. "We may not live in the royal castle, but there's no reason we can't have the most exotic flowers in the land," she said, brushing her palms together. "And soon, my daughter, we might be living in a royal castle after all. While you were out on that horse of yours, you had a gentleman caller. Come to find out, Prince Benjamin is interested in courting you. The only hitch is, he lives way out in Helmsville. For that reason, he'd like to begin courting you while he's still a guest of Queen Eva's. You can't begin to imagine how pleased I am, Regina."

Finally, she let the orchids be and regarded me with an equally discerning eye. Her gaze narrowed on my newly resurrected scar, and my stomach dropped.

With one cold hand, she grabbed me under my chin and directed my face closer to the fiery sconce on the wall.

"What is *that*?" Her voice and eyes were tinged with such disgust I might as well have had a smear of Thaddeus's dung on my nose. She snapped her fingers. "Solomon, your handkerchief."

With a quick step forward, the servant whipped a white square cloth out of his vest pocket. My mother seized it and used it to try to rub off my scar.

"It's there to stay, Mother," I said. "I wished for it."

Her eyes blazed, and as much as I tried not to, I shrank a little.

"You did *what*?"

"I wished on the blue star, and the Blue Fairy granted it with light magic. Not even you can undo it."

She tossed the handkerchief aside, and Solomon practically dove to catch it before it landed on the tiles. "Leave us, Solomon," she ordered through the corner of her lips, and the servant clicked his heels and dutifully made himself scarce.

"I don't understand, Regina. You *wished* for a *scar*?

Did I raise you to be an idiot? Do you *want* to be an old maid?"

"No, Mother. I finally made a decision for *myself*, that's all."

The words were barely out of my mouth when her hand crashed against my cheek. I held back a whimper and stood still—my face stinging and eyes locked on hers. "You're right, Mother. You don't understand."

I turned to look in the silver-framed mirror that had taken the place of our family portrait. "Once upon a time, I was thrown from a horse's back. I didn't let it stop me from doing what I love to do best. The next morning, I got back onto the horse. This," I said, touching the skin above my lip, which now burned from having been rubbed, "is a reminder of how I was able to conquer my greatest fear."

"Perhaps someday you'll be wise enough to make your own decisions, but until then, I'll have to do it for you," she said. In the mirror's reflection, I saw her open her hand. Above her palm hovered a small violet cloud of magic.

As I opened my mouth to protest, my father rounded the corner with a plate of delicious-looking cookies.

His gaze darted from his wife to me and back to his wife again. He abruptly stopped chewing and swallowed with apparent difficulty. "Good gracious, Cora!" he said, stepping between the two of us. "What now? Are you all right, my child?" he asked, his kind brown eyes roaming over my features as he set the plate on the table.

"Yes, Daddy, I'm fine. I'm better than fine."

"Our daughter has injured herself," my mother said, sucking our attention back to her. The cloud of magic grew ominously in her open palm.

I didn't flinch. I refused to be afraid of my mother forever.

He turned to his wife and gently took her hand. She looked down at their entwined fingers as the purple smoke vanished. "Let her be, Cora."

Her mouth dropped open, and she promptly snapped it shut. I was shocked, too, and I could not talk myself into politely averting my eyes. My mother rolled her shoulders back and stretched her arms and fingers down by her sides.

"I was going to fix it like it never happened. It's a shame to have her beautiful face marred in such an unsightly way," she said, frowning. "Particularly now, when she's of the age to be attracting royal suitors. As I'm sure you know, Henry, Prince Benjamin will commence courting Regina tomorrow evening."

"Ah, yes. The prince. I had a nice long chat with him last night. After suffering through monologues about the weather and politics and—oh, yes—how my shoes aren't pointed enough to be in fashion, he thought he'd torture me further with talk of his family."

"So he's not the most skilled conversationalist in the realm," my mother said, twisting her wrist in the air dismissively. "Neither are you, Henry, but I try not to hold it against you."

"Thank you, dear," he said to his wife, giving me a wink on the sly. "However, my point is—and I think the both of you will be interested to know—Benjamin is not of royal blood. He became a prince in title alone by marrying the late Princess Heather of Helmsville. Who, as it turns out, has a rather large family. Three elder sisters and two brothers, one elder and one younger, and all are alive and well."

"So, it would do no good for me to court Prince Benjamin," I said, my sudden glee raising my voice by at least an octave, "let alone wed him."

Shaking her head, my mother slammed her palms on the table. The vase of orchids rocked. "I'm sure that incorrigible Eva relished wasting our time."

"Have you given Benjamin the news I won't be courting him?" I asked my father.

He offered me a cookie. "I presumed you would like to do the honors, my child."

Though my mother glared at me, I bit into the gingersnap. Once I finished, I took another, savoring it. The grandfather clock stuck midnight. "I am going to retire for the night," my mother announced. "Are you coming, Henry?"

"Go ahead, dear. I will join you momentarily."

Her eyes glinted, but she said nothing more. Instead, she turned away from us and made her way to the stairs, her heels clacking on the marble tiles and the sconces and candles flickering in her wake.

Once we were alone, we sat next to each other on the couch. No matter what happened, I knew I would always have my father's love, and he mine. Ever so tenderly, he traced my scar with his finger. "I never thought it possible, but you are fairer than ever before."

His words sent warmth radiating through my whole body. Grinning, I wiped a few cookie crumbs from his beard.

"I'll never forget that day, Regina. I felt so horrible about your accident. I wish it had never happened. I should have never left you, not even for a little while."

"It wasn't your fault. You are not to blame," I said.

"It's a terrible thing when a parent is powerless to keep his child safe. I know you probably don't understand my meaning, but someday, when you are a mother, I know you will."

His words jarred me. Would I, Regina, ever be

somebody's *mother*? Somehow, imagining myself reigning over my own kingdom was easier than imagining myself raising a child. I could only hope I would be a good mother—that my son or daughter would look at me with the kind of love I'd seen reflected in Snow White's eyes in the portrait Jasper had painted of her and Queen Eva.

"Meanwhile," my father resumed, "know I was very proud of you that day. You were very brave. And you still are, Regina."

"I hope you are right." I gave him a hug, and his arms squeezed me for a few seconds even after I'd let go. "Well, it is late, and Mother is waiting for you," I said, happy but weary. I rose and started walking across the living room.

"Regina?"

I turned around.

My father was straightening one of the orchids that had tipped. "Your mother is not so bad. If it weren't for her, Giles wouldn't have had the opportunity to know his niece. Now that he has her, he's straightened himself out. Also, thanks to your mother, you were given the chance to become friends with Claire. I've seen quite a bit of change in you these past few weeks. I know it can be difficult, being somebody's friend. However, I believe you will find it worthwhile."

After I went to my chambers and braided my hair for bed, I paused to examine my scar in the mirror. It was light and small—on the whole, I was sure most everyone would consider it insignificant, if they noticed it at all. Yet to me, it meant so much. It symbolized I could—and would—rise above my fears.

My first order of business in utilizing my rediscovered bravery was getting Claire's ring back for her. *She's done so much for me; it's the least I can do for her.* Snow White had inspired me to emerge from the shadows. The Blue Fairy had given me back a part of my former self. And I, empowered with my renewed sense of courage, intended to retrieve a special part of my dear friend's past for her.

The next day, I would return to the gingerbread cottage.

Twenty

Monday, May 22

My mother kept a close watch on me the entire day. When I'd slipped out to the stables to visit Rocinante after the noonday meal, Jesse had stopped sweeping the planked floor and said, "Your mother has instructed me to alert her if you go out on a ride. I'm to sleep here to ensure you don't take Rocinante out after sunset."

"Let me guess," I'd said. "She wants to keep me safe."

He'd nodded and continued sweeping with feverish urgency. The stables were cleaner and tidier than I'd ever seen, and I guessed my mother had put a fire under his feet—maybe even literally. The horses were off-limits, at least for that night, and Jesse obviously wasn't going to turn a blind eye.

At any rate, I hadn't wanted to alert my mother to anything out of the ordinary, or somehow tip her off that I planned to sneak out and go to the blind witch's cottage. I'd made it a point to stay under her thumb and behave agreeably, even as she flung narrow-eyed stares and underhanded comments about the scar she so reviled.

Later, as I'd climbed into bed, fully clothed, I rationalized that waiting until nighttime had certain advantages. For one, Claire and I could hopefully sneak out of and back in to our respective homes undetected. Furthermore, with any luck, the crotchety witch would be sound asleep, so we could slip into the gingerbread cottage, find Claire's heirloom, and be on our merry way without having to deal with her—or her magic.

In the distance, a wolf howled. The night was warm enough, yet I pulled my cloak around my shoulders to ward off the shivers.

I tossed a handful of gravel at Claire's bedroom window and held my breath. I thought I heard a soft rustle and lifted my lantern. A striped cat prowled over to the hedge, undoubtedly hunting for a midnight meal. Its eyes glowed orange as it slunk along the north side of the mansion, where I stood waiting.

Other than the cat, nothing had stirred. So I grabbed a bigger handful of gravel and threw it with more force. The tiny rocks made an impressive racket against the glass panes. "That will do it," I said to myself. In case I'd inadvertently roused Giles, I hid against the stone wall of the house, out of immediate view from his window.

Claire's blond head appeared in her bedroom window. I leapt back onto the path and waved, then held my finger to my lips so she'd stay quiet. She nodded and disappeared. I returned to the shadows to wait for her to dress and come out, which was quicker than I would have thought possible.

Also wearing a lightweight cloak and holding a lantern, she scurried to my side. "Regina! What in the land? Why are you here? What has gotten into you?"

"*Shhhh!* Come on." I grabbed her by the arm and tugged her along the path, away from her uncle's house and toward the road that led to the royal castle. "Your wish is coming true, Claire. We're going to get your ring back," I said.

She arched her brows. "From the blind witch?"

I nodded. "If she tries to gobble us up, you'll have to set her boots on fire. Then again, Snow said she won't eat us; our meat is too tough." Claire seemed abnormally quiet. I sensed she might be nervous, so a couple of moments later, I added, "However, those boots she was wearing were hideous. You should burn them up anyway."

Claire erupted into what I thought were giggles. Soon, however, I realized my friend wasn't actually laughing at my jest; she was sobbing uncontrollably. She could barely hold her lantern, so I took it for her. "Claire, what's wrong?"

She wiped the tears from her eyes. "Nothing. It's just that this . . . this . . ."—she swept her hand forward, indicating the road to the cottage—"is *so* sweet of you. It means so very much to me. I simply . . ." She sniffled. I waited, but it seemed she could not finish her thought. The fact that she was so touched warmed my heart.

"I'm your friend, aren't I?"

Once she seemed to have stopped the flow of tears, I handed her lantern back to her. Along with our lamps, the stars and the bright crescent moon also helped illuminate our path as Claire and I traipsed through the woods. Soon we came upon the royal stream, and we stopped to drink of it.

I saw something bobbing near the edge of the opposite bank and shone my lantern on it. "Claire, is that an *apple?*" I asked, not believing my eyes.

She leaned forward and tilted her head. "I don't think so."

I passed her my lantern and hopped on a rock to get a better look. "It is!"

"Regina, be careful."

"I'm going to get it," I said, ignoring Claire's warnings. The rock teetered, so I hurriedly jumped onto another and then to one more. When I'd safely made it to the other side, I picked up the apple and let out a yelp. "Claire! I think it's the apple I gave Jasper."

"It can't be," she said as I navigated my way back across. "Goodness, it would be rotten by now. Wouldn't it?"

I misjudged the last step and got my boots and cloak wet, but I did not care. I held the apple in the glow of the lanterns and wiped it clean with my cloak. "I know, it doesn't make sense, but look. It's the same one, as perfect as ever." Cradling it in my hands, I lowered myself onto a log. "Maybe this stream is enchanted. It's the one that flows through the royal gardens. If we were to follow it that way," I said, pointing north, "I believe we would arrive at the bridge where Jasper and I were to meet last Saturday. Are you thinking what I'm thinking, my dear friend?" I could barely catch my breath. When Claire said nothing, I answered on her behalf. "What if Jasper *did* go to the bridge? Perhaps he left the apple for me as a message that he was there, yet couldn't stay? However, I never saw it because it rolled off and was carried downstream. . . . Maybe he cares about me after all."

Claire was listening to me with an odd expression on her face, like she'd bitten into something gristly but swallowed it down to be polite.

"Fair enough," I said, blowing a stream of air up across my forehead. "It's a far-fetched story, the silly stuff of fairy tales."

She gave me a small smile and shrugged her shoulders. "Stranger things have happened."

I slipped the apple into the pocket of my cloak. "Speaking of fairy tales, we have a date with an unsuspecting witch."

Twenty-One

Perhaps it was because it was dark, or because I was nervous about sneaking in uninvited, but the little house seemed to have taken on an even more foreboding appearance than before. The confections looked old and moldy, like the last traces of cheer had been sucked out of them.

"Do you think she's home?" Claire asked as we peered through a slanted sugar-paned window.

A blaze in the fireplace cast a pulsing glow on the witch's living room, yet I couldn't see anyone inside. "She must be in bed," I answered.

I eased open the window, and thankfully, it glided just

high enough for us to slip inside. Claire stepped up, but I signaled for her to allow me to go first. With a shrug, she obliged. As I hoisted myself and climbed through the window, my heart pounded. I took a deep breath, trying to calm my nerves as I waited for her inside. Previously, the cottage had smelled of cakes and sweets; now it had a savory aroma, like roasted lamb.

Claire's feet dropped to the floor, soundless as a cat's paws. The fireplace crackled, flashing light on the back of the witch's head—the familiar blond bird's nest of hair—in the rocking chair. Every muscle in my body tensed, until a series of loud, erratic snores effectively convinced us she was sound asleep.

"Where's the treasure?" Claire whispered.

"The green door," I whispered back, pointing down the hallway. I was more than ready to help Claire find her ring and hurry out of there, never to return again. Then I heard a noise from the kitchen—it almost sounded like pleading whispers—that made me remember how adamant the witch had been that I not peek into it the last time we had been here. So while Claire tiptoed to the back room to look for her ring, I veered off into the kitchen.

As I moved my lamplight around the room, I saw that pans, pots, and bowls cluttered the countertops, table, and sink—and a very large cauldron sat on the floor. Squashes, carrots, and heads of cabbage filled a round reed basket, and sprigs of dried herbs dangled from the rafters. Beneath my feet, dry beans crunched. The kitchen was such a mess, it was no wonder the witch hadn't wanted me to see it.

I scoured the kitchen for the source of the whispers, but neither heard nor saw anything suspicious . . . until I spotted something that looked like a cage in the far corner of the room. Stranger still, when I raised my lantern, I thought I saw something moving behind its spindly bars. However, it must have been the shadows playing tricks on my eyes, because after I blinked and took a closer look, the cage was clearly empty, save for a scrap of plain brown cloth and what appeared to be bread crumbs on its floor. Nonetheless, it was definitely a cage of some kind, plenty big enough to hold a goat, a pig, or a large dog. Or . . . a child, as Snow White's nightmarish bedtime story had suggested. I felt a chill run through me.

A blind witch that eats children?

It was too absurd to believe. Laughable, really. I smiled to myself, but the expression felt forced. On the back side of the table, next to the oven, there was a pile of bones. Some of them were picked clean, but a few had bits of meat stuck to them. Animal bones, surely.

"What are you doing?" Claire said in a harsh whisper. She startled me so, it was a wonder I didn't leap straight out of my shoes.

"Oh my goodness, you scared the dickens out of me! I thought you were *her*," I said as soon as I found my voice.

"No, she's still asleep. Can't you hear her?" Claire paused, and sure enough, the blind witch emitted a snore loud enough to be heard at the royal castle. "You were right, Regina. That room is full of all sorts of treasure. I've never seen anything like it."

"Did you find the ring?"

"I did. . . ." She must have sensed something was wrong, because she stopped talking and raised her lantern. Its glow skirted over the pile of bones and rested on what appeared to be a skull. It looked like the human skulls sketched in my learning books, only it was smaller.

"Oh my goodness, Regina," Claire gasped. "Is that . . . ?"

Snow White's voice sounded in my ears, as if she were standing beside us: *She lures children into her house and fattens them up. And then,* she eats them up for supper!

I screamed.

Claire's eyes widened and she dropped the lantern. "No!" She pushed her hand over my mouth, trying to smother my screams. *"Shhhhh!"* Shadows bounced and danced around the kitchen, making it seem like everything around us—the pots, bowls, knives, and chairs—were enchanted and coming to attack us. My knees gave out. I reached for the table to catch myself, smashing a platter and the cookies that had been stacked on it.

"Who goes there?"

The witch's voice sent a shiver down my spine. She stood in the doorway, her hands straight out in front of her and black makeup smeared down her cheeks and all around her cloudy eyes. Claire stepped back into the pile of bones. As each bone slipped and slid, it made a telltale clacking noise. It was an ominous beat, reminiscent of the drummers at a public execution mere seconds before the headsman lowered the ax.

"I know you," said the witch, flaring her nostrils. "I'd recognize that vile stench of rose water anywhere." She tittered for a second or two and then stopped abruptly. "No good. Too old, too old for me. I warned you never to come back, yet here you are, uninvited. Eating my precious cookies. Harassing a poor blind woman. Oh, but there's more. . . ." She closed the distance between herself and Claire, navigating around the cauldron and other obstacles with incredible precision. "I smell a thief. You've come to *rob* me, haven't you? Speak up, girl. I cannot hear you. Confess!"

Claire cleared her throat, yet her voice still wavered.

"No, you're mistaken. We simply left something behind we had to return for."

"Liar," the witch growled, assailing us with her foul breath. "If your pockets are empty, I will allow you to leave in peace. If not . . ." She flexed one of her talons, making a sickening popping noise. Claire shifted out of her reach just long enough to pass me the ring. My mind whirred and my eyes darted all around, trying to formulate a plan to get us out of there without a repeat of the miniature tornado, or any other magical mayhem she chose to craft.

Claire grimaced and squirmed as the witch patted her down, until finally, she spoke. "I haven't anything of yours."

The witch grunted in frustration. She whirled around to face me and spat, "Are *you* the burglar? What have you to say, girl?"

"You are correct. I stole something," I said as calmly as possible as I untied the ribbon from my braid and looped it around the ring. "But only one thing. A gold ring with a quality red garnet in it. I'm sure it's worth quite a bit."

"Does the gold form a dragon's claw?"

Claire shook her head at me like I'd lost my mind, and in all honesty, she was probably right. I couldn't very well back out now, though.

"Indeed," I said.

The witch smacked her deep red lips and reached out her hand. "Give it to me."

I tossed the ring high into the air, the ribbon trailing behind it like a May Day streamer. It landed with a small *thunk* in the center of the cage. "Get it yourself," I said.

Claire edged closer to the cage, holding the door ajar in preparation.

The woman laughed wheezily and mumbled something about "thieving girls" before bolting after the ring. At the same instant she crouched down to grab it, Claire slammed the door shut and, holding it in place, said, "There's the key on that peg."

I stuck the key into its slot and twisted, but the witch

flicked her free hand and the key flew out, narrowly missing my ear as it hurtled across the kitchen. The witch rubbed Claire's ring to her cheek as if nuzzling a baby bunny. Claire tried to yank it away with the ribbon, but the witch's hold was too strong.

"Forget about the ring," I said to Claire. "Let's get out of here." Suddenly, the bunches of herbs dropped from the ceiling and a dozen knives shot out of the wooden block on the counter, pinning me to the floor by the hem of my cloak. When I tried to untie it at my neckline, the knot magically tightened over and over again.

I reached into my pocket, grabbed the apple, and flung it at the witch as hard as I could. It flew between the bars and struck her between her unseeing eyes. Screeching, the woman pawed at the air, giving Claire the perfect opportunity to reclaim her ring. I braced myself for the witch to use magic to snatch the ring back again, but instead, she picked up the apple and held it to her lips. She didn't take a bite, though. "Where did you get this?" she demanded, holding it against the cage.

"I don't know. I, uh, found it," I said, trying to reach a pot or pan—or anything that could be used as a weapon. But everything was out of my reach.

"Well, it's no matter. Now you've lost it. *I've* found it, and finders keepers." She gently—almost lovingly—ran her fingers over the apple, humming.

I desperately wiggled and tugged at one of the knives, trying to pull it out of the floor. "*Do* something," I urged Claire.

"What would you have me do?" she asked, pushing her weight against the door to keep the witch imprisoned.

The knife finally gave, and I cut through my cloak. Luckily, the witch was too preoccupied with the apple to realize I was free. "Use your magic."

"Regina, I . . ."

Stepping over the heap of my ruined cloak, I grabbed the broom from the wall beside me and readied myself for battle.

The witch shot a very heated, sightless glare at me. "Foolish girl, can't you see? She hasn't magic." With that, the door of the cage burst open with incredible force.

Claire tumbled hard to the floor, right at my feet. The ring soared magically into the air, falling onto the witch's ready finger. "It's no matter," said the witch. "She'll still pay the price."

I dropped the broom. "Claire!" I cried, trying to help her up. "What are you waiting for?"

My friend squinted her eyes, as if she didn't know me—as if she didn't comprehend the gravity of our situation, or how much we needed her to fight the witch's magic with her own.

"Did you hit your head? What is wrong?"

She gasped. "Cora?"

"No, it's me . . . Regina. Claire, you're scaring me."

"Please . . ." Tears blurred Claire's pretty blue eyes, and she shifted her feet on the floor, prying off one of her shoes.

Freed from the cage, the witch hovered over us, waiting—for what, I had no idea. I had the ominous feeling that any second, she would do something horrible to us.

Unfortunately, I was right.

No sooner had Claire whispered another "please" than a strong gust blew me into the cage where the witch had been squatting only moments ago. I rolled up against the far wall, my spine slamming into the iron bars. Pain zapped through my body, and when I lunged for the door, it slammed in my face and locked with a resounding *click*. The witch's dark red lips furled, and she triumphantly clutched the apple to her bosom.

I had to do something, and fast. I couldn't let the blind witch best me again, and moreover, Claire needed my help. Behind the spindly bars, I felt the chilling fear her juvenile prisoners must have experienced when they were trapped in there, not knowing what would become of them. Lucky for me, my meat was too old and tough for her taste. Suddenly, I had an idea.

"I wonder when those two pudgy children will be passing by," I said, and the witch tilted her head as I laid out the crumbs of my story in my mind. "I didn't recognize them, the poor dears. Didn't their parents tell them tales of big, bad wolves and terrible ogres to keep them from venturing into the woods at this time of night?

Maybe you know them: a little boy who's clearly never skipped his dessert, and a rosy-cheeked girl in pigtails."

The witched smacked her dark red lips. "Children, you say? Heading *here*? But I am not prepared. Oh, I have so much to do—so very, very much!" she cried. She dropped the apple on the countertop and started moving dishes and food around, feverishly trying to tidy up.

"They've likely been snagged by a wolf," I said.

"What if they haven't? What if they're on their way? What if those two delicious children will be traipsing by at any moment?"

"Even if they are, and even if they stop to indulge in your candies, cakes, and treats, it's too bad this cage is already full."

"You! Get out. Make room." The witch charged at me, shaking the cage with her gnarled hands.

I crossed my arms and raised my chin defiantly, but I remembered the witch couldn't see my acting. Instead, I held my finger to my lips, gesturing for Claire to remain quiet. My poor disoriented friend didn't seem to be following, and I didn't want her to speak up and ruin my yarn. "I don't *want* to get out," I said. "It's rather pleasant in here; and besides, it's late and I'm weary. This is a perfect place to get a good night's sleep, and my friend is fine on your floor, as well."

"Get out," the witch said vehemently. She raised her hand and the door of the cage swung open with such force I felt my body being pulled toward it. Her cloudy eyes rolled side to side in their sockets. She began chanting a string of indecipherable words—some kind of spell, I presumed—and the kitchen, along with the sliver of the living room viewable from the cage, returned to its former glory. Elegant candelabra cast an inviting glow on plates stacked high with the most delicious-looking and -smelling goodies, and all evidence of what would become of her victims—save the cage I was still in—had vanished without a trace. The result was convincing enough to make me forget about the witch's unappealing habit of devouring children, at least for two or three seconds.

"I'll make a deal with you," I said, bracing myself.

The witch brushed her hands together. "Mmmm? What kind of deal?"

"We will leave your house immediately, *if* you let us go in peace, and *if* you give my friend her ring."

"You won't interfere with the children?" she asked, twisting the ring on her grotesquely gnarled finger.

I shook my head, again having forgotten she couldn't see me. "You have my word."

"And I can keep the apple?"

"If you insist," I said.

"For whom was it intended? Tell me."

"Why does it matter? It's yours now."

"It matters because it's a poison apple. You have eyes, but you don't know a poison apple when you see it? Whoever bites into this fruit will fall into a deep, deep sleep. The only thing that can awaken them is a kiss from their true love. A romantic tale if it turns out that way, a tragic one if it doesn't."

I'd already suspected the witch was mad, but her latest rant only proved it. "Do we have a deal?"

"Indeed, we do." She held the gold-and-garnet ring out for me to take as I wriggled out of the cage.

I yanked Claire off the floor, scooped up her shoe,

and darted as quickly as I could to the front door while dragging her along. Behind us, the witch called, "You'll never set foot in my cottage again, thieves. Only succulent little boys and girls. Juicy, tender little children, no one else. This time I'll cast a spell to make sure of it. Don't return, or you will be sorry."

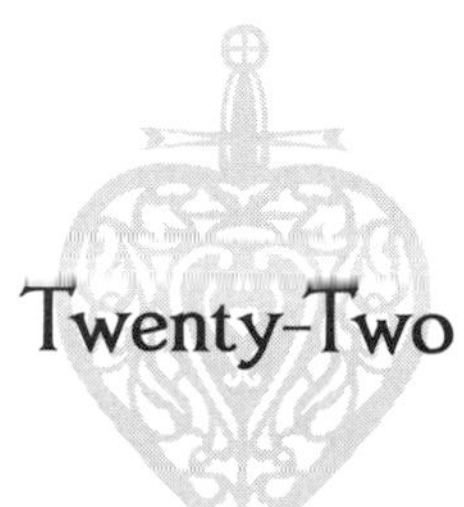

Twenty-Two

Tuesday, May 23

"My niece is in bed," Giles said apologetically when I showed up at his door. It was a little past ten in the morning, so I figured our adventure with the blind witch had worn Claire out. I might not have been out and about, either, had I not been eager to give Claire the ring I'd mistakenly kept when I'd dropped her off at home late the night before.

Though it had only been gently sprinkling when Rocinante and I first left, now the clouds were leaking fat, sluggish raindrops. *Hopefully, by the time I leave here, the storm will have blown over, and it will turn out to be a beautiful day,*

I mused as Giles invited me inside. If so, maybe I could talk Claire into joining me on a longer ride that afternoon. Perhaps we could return to the pond and work on magic. I could think of nothing better than celebrating our victory over the blind witch by spending the entire day with my friend.

"What happened here?" Giles asked, pointing at my lip. "Would you like something for it? It's already scarred, but a little salve might make it less apparent."

"Thank you, but it is all right as it is," I said. He leaned forward, his eyes squinting in curiosity, as if he might be remembering the cut my mother had magically healed after he'd left our house that day so long ago. I quickly changed the topic back to Claire. "I slept in longer than usual this morning, too. It must be something to do with our age, or perhaps the weather?"

"Actually, Claire has quite a bump on her head," Giles said. I frowned and nodded sympathetically as he relayed what Claire had obviously told him. "She was walking in her sleep last night and fell. I'm sure she'll be glad you've come by. However, I've instructed her to rest as much as possible, and I'd appreciate your cooperation."

"I understand. I won't be long," I said, growing concerned.

When I opened the door to Claire's bedroom a moment later, she was sitting arrow-straight in her bed, staring at the wall in front of her. When she turned toward me, it was as if her neck were made of wood. A bandage was wrapped around her head, a crown fashioned of white cloth. Her eyes closed and opened halfway, and she exhaled loudly. "I'm fine," she said, before I could ask. "My uncle is overly cautious with me, that's all. I'll be good as new tomorrow, to be sure."

"I'm glad to hear it," I said, tentatively approaching her. Again, she turned her gaze to the wall. "I brought you something." I'd strung her brother's ring on one of my gold chains, and now I fastened it around her neck.

"Thank you, Regina." Her eyes welled up as she caressed her heirloom. "You're such a good friend to me."

I slipped off my boots and sat next to her on the

bed. "Now you'll have something of your brother's to pass down to your firstborn," I said, straightening her necklace for her. The wonderful feeling that flowed over me must've been what friendship was all about. Knowing Claire was happy made *me* happy. "Who knows, maybe it will be your uncle who delivers for you, and if I'm lucky, I'll get to be there, too, to help welcome your baby into the land."

"Our children can grow up together, and be friends as we are. . . ." Her voice trailed off, and she slowly bowed her head. I had the terrible sinking feeling her injury was far more serious than she'd let on.

"Claire, what's wrong? Are you dizzy? Sick to your stomach? Do you want me to get Giles for you?"

She lifted her head and blinked sleepily. "No, no. I'll be all right."

"You must have hit your head harder than I thought you did. I've a mind to go back and make that witch pay for hurting you so. This time, you really can set her boots aflame." Not only was I angry with the witch for having hurt Claire, but I was also selfishly upset to have to wait for my friend to feel well enough to spend time with me. It had been less than five minutes, and I already missed the old Claire. "Alternately, you can teach *me* how to do the magic, and I'll do it myself."

She licked her pale lips. "I have a confession," she said in a soft, somber tone. "I'm scared to death to tell you. However, I cannot go on like this. You're such a wonderful friend to me."

"What is it?" I took her hand in mine. It felt cold, and somehow smaller than before. "You can tell me anything, Claire. Anything except that you're going home to Port Bennett. I don't know what I'd do with myself if you lived such a great distance from me." I rubbed her hand to warm it up.

She slipped her hand away and held it awkwardly above her knees. "I do not have magic."

"What are you talking about? Yes, you do." I scooted to the edge of the mattress. "I'm going to go fetch Giles and have him reexamine your head."

Claire squeezed my shoulder. "Regina, please. Stay. I need you to hear me. I don't have magic. I never did."

"No need to be humble, Claire. I saw you light that man's boots on fire at the market, remember? Even if you aren't the most powerful mage in the Enchanted Forest, you'll get there. You once told me magic can't be rushed. Remember?"

She studied her hands in a most disturbing way—as if she'd never seen them before. She swallowed and winced, like her throat was sore. "It wasn't my magic," she whispered.

"Wasn't your magic . . . ?" I repeated, churning the thought around in my mind. "Whose magic was it, then?" The room suddenly appeared dimmer than before, but the candles on Claire's bureau were still lit. I could only presume the clouds were blackening, preparing for a powerful storm.

"Claire? Answer me!"

She clamped down on her trembling bottom lip. "Cora's," she said in a whisper.

I shook my head, certain I'd misheard her. "What did you say?"

"Your mother's," she said, a little louder. Her face blanched.

"No. *No.*" In my mind's eye, I saw the orchids in our foyer back home, changing from light pink, to deep pink, and finally, to crimson. There was suddenly a sharp ache in the pit of my stomach. "You're telling me it was my *mother's* magic?"

Claire nodded her head once. "She was in the marketplace with us. She'd cast a glamour spell on herself so she'd appear to be a common villager," she choked out.

This made no sense to me. I planted my feet on the floor and stood. Freed from my weight, the mattress sprang up. "I don't understand. Why would my mother want me to believe you had magic?"

Though our gazes connected at that instant, Claire's seemed to focus on something other than me, something beyond her window and the rain that was beginning to shower down. Something bigger. Something painful.

"Because she loves you, Regina. She wants to protect you."

My thoughts were so jumbled I physically shook my head in a futile attempt to align them. "If you never had magic, what about the lessons you gave me . . . ?"

"They were only a ploy." She took a deep, shaky breath before continuing. "Oh, Regina, I am so sorry. If you could have seen your face, how excited you were when you thought you'd used magic to knock the frog off its lily pad. I truly wished it had been real." She briefly closed her eyes and then turned her gaze to her lap. "When you confided in me that you wanted to learn magic, your mother wanted to give you a wee taste—enough to keep your hope alive, to keep your mind off going straight to her source. She told me the one who taught *her* magic is a contemptible beast. Since the two of them have such a dark and sordid past, she wanted to keep you away from him—and others like him—at all costs. So, that's why she made me pretend to know magic."

I wrung my hands and paced around the floor. "I don't understand, Claire. Why did you tell my mother

I wished to learn magic in the first place? You knew I didn't want her privy to that. You assured me she never would be." I suddenly felt like I were teetering on the ledge of a cliff.

She fidgeted for a few seconds, keeping me in suspense. And when she finally spoke, her words were oddly stilted. "When Cora came to Port Bennett and offered me an introduction to high society, I jumped at the chance. Not only did she give me a way out of Port Bennett—and away from the lowlifes who tormented me on a daily basis—she presented me the opportunity to know my uncle. My ma had always spoken so highly of him, even though the only men I've ever known have hurt us, with the exception of my brother." She paused, tracing the contour of her ring with the pad of her thumb. "Furthermore, I knew if I lived at my uncle's estate, I'd have a much better chance to make the sort of connections that would help me take care of my ma in the future, as it seems each day of keeping the tavern afloat strips an entire year off her life."

"You made a deal with my mother," I said, practically

spitting the words. "On her end, she brought you here and gave you the chance to better your life. On your end, all you had to do was pretend to be my friend and report to her everything I did and every word I said."

"Yes, but—"

Something snapped deep inside me, and when I laughed, it sounded strangely dark to my own ears. "Well. I'm disappointed in you, Claire. You could have asked for so much more. You should have asked my mother to spin some straw into gold for you." I balled my hands into fists. "That would set you and your ma up quite nicely, don't you agree? As for 'connections,' you could have asked her to make you so beautiful and graceful, no nobleman would be able to resist you. Or, since you enjoy writing stories in your aunt's old journals, you could have asked my mother to make you a famous author. I'm sure there's a spell for that, and after all, Cora is a powerful sorceress."

With each word I spat out, Claire winced, and I thought that maybe, somewhere deep inside myself, I did, as well.

I sat on a stool by the window and buried my face in my hands. I thought about all the times we'd had together. All the adventures on horses, in the royal castle, and at the gingerbread cottage. All the quiet moments we'd had in the drawing room, in my bedroom, and in Snow White's chamber. The way she'd spoken up to my mother in my favor. And, of course, the ostensible magic lessons.

"Regina, I am so sorry. I wish I'd never made the deal. If only I could turn back the hands of the clock . . ."

I had been tricked, and with every memory that passed through my mind—flashbacks that used to fill my heart with warmth, love, and hope—I tightened my fists, until I was sure my fingernails would puncture my palms and draw blood. For some strange and eerily dark reason, the idea of bleeding sounded good to me.

"It was all a sham," I said through gritted teeth. "A lie. Everything. You are nothing but my mother's pawn."

Claire shook her head emphatically as she rolled out of bed. She stood on the rug in her nightdress and bare feet. Her entire body seemed to shrink and wither like a rotting apple. "Not everything was a lie, Regina. Please believe me. Cora may be the reason we met in the first place, but our friendship . . . it is real."

Oh, how I wanted to believe in our friendship! I hadn't even realized I'd been pacing until I came to an abrupt stop at the foot of the bed. "You may think you know what my mother is capable of, what she'll do to make sure nothing—and *no one*—gets in the way of my becoming queen. But you have no idea."

"I know Cora is powerful, but she only wants the best for you. So do I." She closed the space between us and reached for my hand.

I yanked it away and raked my fingers through my hair. "Please stop saying that. You've proven where your loyalty lies." I crossed my arms over my chest. My heart thumped hard within my rib cage.

"I'm not loyal to your mother, Regina. I'm afraid of her."

"Well, now you know how I feel," I harrumphed.

Claire wiped her face with the back of her hand, and

I flexed my jaw, reminding myself that no matter how pitiful and remorseful she appeared, she'd been aligned with my mother all along. She was a traitor, and I didn't know how or when, but I was going to make her pay . . . and pay dearly.

"Oh, Regina," Claire said between sniffles, "I would have chosen to be your friend, even if Cora hadn't taken my heart. You're the best friend I've ever had. The best I've ever even dreamed of having."

I was gathering my boots to leave when something she'd said stuck in me like a barbed thorn. "My mother . . . took your heart?"

Twenty-Three

A memory from when I was twelve seeped into the forefront of my mind. Hwin was lying in her stall on her side, dead. Jesse was sweeping. The bristles of his broom were coated with dark red dust. I didn't know what the memory meant, but something deep inside of me told me this time, Claire was telling the truth.

My own heart felt like it was pumping rocks rather than blood. "What are you talking about?"

She grabbed my hand and placed it on the left side of her chest. I closed my eyes, waiting for the telltale thump of a heart through her nightgown. I felt nothing but the erratic trembles of Claire's sobs.

My head was spinning. "I don't understand. How can you still be alive if you haven't a heart?"

"She said it was her favorite—and most evil—spell of all," Claire explained. "When she has somebody's heart in her possession, she can, at any given moment, squeeze it, causing excruciating pain—or worse, smash it, turning it to dust."

The floor of Claire's bedroom seemed to fall. I collapsed to my knees as my mind pieced together the puzzle. My mother had murdered Hwin. In the name of protecting me—or perhaps in an act of revenge—she'd ripped the mare's heart out of her body and crushed it into a powder. The image of Jesse sweeping away the dark red dust played over and over again in my mind's eye.

Now my mother had Claire's heart. "At any given moment, my mother can kill you," I whispered.

Claire nodded. With the heel of her hand, she futilely wiped her tear-streaked face. "The day she walked into ma's tavern, I agreed to keep an eye on you and report back to her with anything that seemed dangerous or suspicious to your well-being or well-breeding. Basically, she wanted me to be her eyes and ears, to help her protect you.

"It was all right at first, and to be honest, I was envious your mother cared enough to keep such a close eye on you. When you confided in me you wished to learn magic, I told her. She came undone, blaming me for putting the dangerous notion in your head. She said it was too great a risk to allow our friendship to continue, and threatened to get Uncle Giles to send me home straightaway. I didn't know how she would make him do that, but I knew better than to underestimate her power.

"I begged her to let me stay. I didn't want to go back to Port Bennett. Furthermore, I wanted to stay, because of *you*, Regina. Because of our friendship. When I told Cora this, she said it was a good thing I'd caught her on a good day, and she'd strike another deal with me. She'd let me stay here, and allow me to remain friends with you, but in order to protect you, she had to take precautions. Of course, I didn't realize what she meant, exactly, until the day before I brought you to the marketplace. I showed up at your door to see if you'd like to go on a horseback ride, but Cora said you'd already gone on one. She expected you back shortly, so she invited me into the library to wait for you to return. That's when she closed the door and . . ."

"Ripped your heart out," I finished when she seemed incapable of doing so herself. Having uttered those four words out loud made it horribly, gut-wrenchingly real, and I wished I had remained silent.

Claire nodded. After blinking several times, she forged on. "Cora is going to give my heart back. She promised." She walked over to the windows and wedged open the square one in the center. "Then again, maybe not," she added, paying no mind to the rain spilling in and pooling on the sill. "Maybe she will crush it, to punish me for confessing all of this to you now."

Claire clutched her chest and began breathing arduously. I rose on shaky legs and rushed over to her, stopping short by a couple of paces. "Claire, are you all right?" I asked.

Claire's life was literally in my mother's hands. The horrific thought filled every part of my body, tensing my muscles until they ached and burned. "Is my mother crushing your heart right now?" I asked. I felt hurt, confused, and scorched by Claire's betrayal, but I did not wish her *dead*. I surely didn't want to watch her die.

Claire dropped her hand from her chest and caught herself on the windowsill. Rainwater trickled from the flooded ledge, splatting on the stone floor and wetting her feet. "I'm all right," she said, her tone tinged with disbelief.

On quivering legs, I made my way over to her vanity to find her a handkerchief. When I opened the drawer, I spotted a piece of parchment, and on it was a familiar signature.

I reached for it just as Giles entered the room. Through his round wire-rimmed glasses, he peered first at his niece, then at me, then back at her again. "Is everything all right, Claire?" he asked, his voice pitched with worry. "Please, lie down. You're overexerting yourself. And Regina," he said, facing me only a split second after I'd slipped the letter into my pocket, "thank you for coming by. You're welcome to wait out the storm in the comfort of my living room. The fire is stoked and biscuits are laid out." He nodded, polite yet stern.

"I will see myself out, thank you," I said as levelly as possible. Turning my back to them, I pulled on my boots and darted out of Claire's chambers and through Giles's enormous hall—my eyes too blurry with looming tears to distinguish any of his furniture, artwork, or servants. Everything had been reduced to a streak of muted colors, whirling around me like a windmill.

When I ran outside and saw my beautiful steed waiting for me—so faithful and strong—I collapsed into him, shaking. The cool rain washed down my hair and back as I buried my nose in his mane. I could have stayed there forever, breathing in my favorite smell, but I needed to get away from Claire. I needed time to contemplate what she'd told me, everything from the deal she'd willingly made with my mother before I'd met her, to now, when her heart was in my mother's hands.

"Regina," Claire cried from the front door. "Please, let's talk. There's more."

Turning my back to her, I fished the letter out of my pocket.

Dear Regina,

I'm sorry to disappoint you tonight. I never wanted to hurt you, but I cannot in good conscience allow you to believe there is something between us when my heart belongs to someone else. I am returning the perfect apple you gave me, as I am far too imperfect to have it. I hope you find your happily ever after.

~ Jasper B. Holding

A mixture of rain and tears dampened the paper, smudging the ink. In no time, every last word he'd written became nothing but a black smear, and the paper began falling apart.

"What did you do?" I asked, holding the soggy letter up in the air. "Go to the bridge, steal the letter meant for me, and toss the apple—also meant for me—into the river, hoping I'd never know the truth?"

"I had to get rid of the apple, Regina. It was cursed. Whoever bit into it would fall into a deep sleep, only to be awakened by True Love's Kiss. I honestly did not know until Cora told me what she'd done—"

I didn't care to hear the rest of her explanation. With the help of the dream I'd had the night before my final lesson with Jasper, I realized my mother's evil plan. She'd meant for Jasper to eat it, and when my kiss wouldn't break the spell, I'd find out the hard way I was not his true love. His heart belonged to someone else, as he'd written in his letter. He was in love with the girl in the head bandage, nightdress, and bare feet. The one I used to call my friend.

"I wanted to spare your feelings, Regina. I couldn't bear for him to break your heart," she said through the rain.

"Don't you realize *you've* broken it?"

All I could think of was getting as far away from

Claire Fairchild as possible. Once my tears started spilling, they blinded me. To make matters worse, the slippery rope and my shaky hands made the task of untethering Rocinante a real challenge.

From behind Claire, I heard Giles beckoning for her to come back indoors. He had his hand on her shoulder and was guiding her back into his house.

"Please, come wait in here, at least until the rain stops," Claire begged.

My throat tightened, and I wished to go back in time, to when no matter how insufferable my life had seemed to be, Claire had been there to shine hope on my path. But as Giles finally succeeded in getting his niece inside and closing the door, I knew everything had changed.

Luckily, the knot finally came loose, and without so much as a glance back at Giles's house, I climbed into the saddle. As Rocinante worked up to a gallop, I cursed the mud, the rain, the tree that had toppled over and blocked the road, my mother, and Claire. Most of all, I cursed myself.

How could I have been so naive? How could I have believed Claire was truly my friend? How could I have opened my heart to her? And when everything came crashing down, how could I have allowed myself to cry in front of her?

All my life, I'd hated feeling frightened. Now I realized I hated feeling vulnerable even more. It was as if someone were hollowing me out with the apple corer Rainy used when she baked cobbler or tarts.

As my home came into view, I stopped crying and set my jaw, knowing what I had to do.

Twenty-Four

After leaving Rocinante in Jesse's hands, I slipped into the foyer past a stony, sleepy Solomon. The door to my father's smoking room was ajar, spilling a slat of light into the hallway. I thought of when I was six, when he'd invited me to sit on his lap and told me that tale about the old man and the snake. The man had continued to feed the snake, even after it had filled him with deadly venom. Biting the man was in his nature, the snake had explained. The story made sense to me now.

I stormed past the smoking room without glancing inside. The maid, who was in the midst of mopping the landing, jumped, obviously startled.

"Where is my mother?" I asked.

Her gaze dropped to the trail of muddy footprints I'd left on the tiles. "Her Highness took her morning meal in her chambers," she said, her tone pleasant but her face flushed.

Not bothering to remove my boots, I tromped up to my room, stomping and grinding mud into the snake woven into my rug. Next I headed to my parents' quarters. Instead of knocking first, I swung open the double doors, finding my mother in one of the high-backed forest green and violet chairs of her reading nook.

I expected her to say something about the unacceptability of barging in, but she simply nodded a greeting, as if she'd been expecting me. The impression of her slender body quickly disappeared from the lush cushions as she stood. "I do enjoy a good read on a rainy day," she said, crossing the enormous room and tucking her tome under her pillow on the bed.

April, eleven years earlier

Lightning flashed and thunder crashed. Rain pelted and lashed my windows angrily. I covered my head with my blankets, but each time I peeked out, the shadows were still there, swarming my bedroom like soul-hungry wraiths.

"It's going to be fine, Isabella," I told my favorite doll. "There is nothing to be afraid of."

She stared at me, her big dark eyes glinting and the hint of a smile on her rosebud lips. I could tell she didn't believe me. "Fine," I said. "Let's go."

Hugging Isabella close, I scurried down the long, dimly lit hallway to my parents' chambers and, with my shoulder, nudged open the enormous double door.

"What is it, Regina?" My mother's voice came over my father's snores.

"May we sleep with you? Just for a little while?" I asked.

"Don't tell me you're scared, Regina. Not even that incorrigible mutt of your father's is afraid of the thunder."

She waved her long fingernails at the hound-shaped lump at Daddy's feet.

"I'm not scared, but Isabella is. So, may we? Please, Mother."

She sighed. "Very well, but only until the storm passes."

I wiggled under the covers and tucked my doll next to me, making sure her tiny tiara didn't snag the fine linens. The lightning seemed even bigger from my parents' giant windows, but thankfully, the shadows looked nothing like wraiths, soul-hungry or otherwise.

Maybe if I play like I'm asleep, she'll allow me to stay here all night, I thought as I plumped my pillow. I shut my eyes tightly and breathed deeply, smelling my mother's new lotion and Thaddeus's doggy breath and hearing my father's loud snores and soft wheezes.

Several minutes later, when my mother's snores offset my father's, I reached out to cuddle Isabella, only to discover she was gone! I opened my eyes and bolted upright. Thank goodness, she wasn't missing after all. She'd merely fallen to the floor. The bottom of her shiny pink gown poked out from beneath the bed. I rolled over to my belly and reached for her.

"Regina, what are you doing?"

"Wh-what's going on?" my father asked, floundering to a sitting position.

Mother said calmly, "Nothing, Henry. Go back to sleep. Regina was frightened of the storm, so I allowed her to sleep in here until it passes."

My father grinned sleepily, and as his head hit the pillow, he mumbled, "You're a good mother, Cora, my darling."

"May we sleep with you the whole night through?" I asked my mother as I picked Isabella off the floor and tucked her in again.

"The storm is over," she answered, even though it was thundering and raining as much as ever. "Come now, Regina. I will walk you back to your room."

Before I knew it, Mother had me by my hand and I had Isabella by hers, and we were being dragged to my bedroom.

"Good night, Regina."

I obediently climbed into my bed. "Good night, Mother." I covered Isabella's head so she wouldn't see the wraith shadows, and I covered mine, as well, so she wouldn't feel all alone.

At some point that night, I heard an unusual noise, and I lowered the blanket off my face so I could take a peek. I thought it was probably a wraith that had returned for me, but it wasn't. It was Mother, lying next to me, snoring softly.

Tuesday, May 23

Lightning struck, illuminating every detail of my parents' majestic bedroom for a split second. I felt my mother's eyes rove over me, from my wet, matted hair to my soiled clothes and, finally, my stockinged feet.

"Regina, what in the land happened to you?" A crinkle appeared atop the bridge of her nose, making her appear more disgusted than worried. "Have you any idea how *filthy* you are?" She straightened the gold-and-crimson tassels on her pillow. "Where have you been?"

I stepped closer to her, trying to ignore the buckling sensation in my knees. "You know where I've been, Mother."

She arched an eyebrow. "What is your meaning, Regina? Out with it, and mind your tone. I have a busy day ahead of me."

Whimpering, Thaddeus leapt off the bed, landing with a *thunk*, and waddled as fast as he could for the door. Part of me—almost every single part of me, truth be told—wanted to follow him. However, it was as if my feet were nailed to the floor. I swallowed hard and choked out the words, "You have Claire's heart."

A darkness eclipsed her eyes until they were as good as black. I braced myself for whatever spell she was going to cast on me, but when she lifted her hands, she merely smoothed her hair. She padded to her bureau and slid open the top middle drawer. Then she withdrew a small wooden box with pinecones carved into it and flipped up its top. "I'm surprised it took you so long to figure it out," she said. "I'd thought my daughter was smarter than that."

As her fingers splayed around the bright red organ, I clasped my hand over my mouth to keep from screaming. It was as if the heart she held in her hand were my own. It beat slow and steady, and I was at once horrified to see it and relieved to know it was still full of life. It took me a while to look away from it, and even longer to meet her gaze.

My mother seemed to be thoroughly scrutinizing my reaction, possibly even enjoying herself. Her head tilted and her left brow arched, and the faintest of smiles graced her lips.

"How . . . how could you do that to somebody?" I asked.

"I'm your mother." She placed the heart in the box and put it back in its drawer, as if it were merely a necklace or a diary. "It is my job to protect you."

"Forgive me for not feeling grateful," I said, blinking and glancing off to the corner of the room to keep from crying. In a single day, I felt like I'd shed more tears than I should in an entire lifetime.

"You blamed me for your not having any companions, so I gave you one," my mother said with a casual shrug. "It was a gift. You *should* be grateful."

"But—"

She rolled right over my protest, her voice rising. "Magic is not something to be taken lightly, Regina. Once you crack open that door, there is no closing it." She slammed the drawer shut, shoving the wooden box and its ghastly contents into the depths of her bureau.

"Are you going to keep her heart in that box?" I asked.

"What would you have me do? Crush it?" She rubbed her hands together. "No, no. Too messy. Besides, it would take a toll on your father if Giles had to mourn yet another death in his pitiful little family. Though I have to say, your friend is lucky," she said, running her fingers along the arch of her bureau. "I don't usually show mercy to those who don't hold up their end of the deal."

"She's not my friend," I said, crossing my arms over my chest. "I want her out of my life. However, she won't be, as long as you have her heart in your possession. You *are* going to return it to her, aren't you?"

"I suppose she does need it back at some point," my mother said, primping her hair in the bureau mirror. It dawned on me that if it were up to her, she'd leave the heart in the box for all eternity. For all I knew, she had an entire collection of people's hearts. It was a thought that made me shudder.

"What will it cost me to get it back for her?" I asked.

"An interesting question, Regina." She held my gaze in the mirror's reflection. "What are you willing to give me in exchange for Claire's heart?"

I set my jaw. "I will return the poison apple to you."

If she was shocked I knew of the curse, or surprised that Jasper hadn't eaten the apple after all, she did a commendable job keeping her features steady.

"I couldn't care less about that piece of fruit. But don't be disheartened, my dear. Give it some more thought, and let me know when you're ready to make a deal."

Though I felt like my bones had turned to pudding, I squared my shoulders and turned to leave. "I shall."

"Regina?"

"Yes, Mother?"

She arched her left eyebrow. "What do you care whether Claire has her heart or not?"

"An interesting question, Mother," I said, and then shut her door.

Later that evening, as I sat down at my vanity and grabbed my brush, I stopped to check my reflection in the mirror. I appeared different, somehow—and not because of the scar above my lip. It was something else, something bigger: the combined effect of my dark hair flowing past my shoulders, my lips curved up ever so slightly, my piercing, unflinching eyes. It was as if my mother were looking at me through the glass.

Tomorrow would be the day I faced my biggest fear. "I'm ready to make a deal she cannot refuse," I said to my reflection.

Twenty-Five

Wednesday, May 24

I knocked on the door to my mother's office. Her voice called, "Enter, Regina."

Though I'd scarcely slept a wink the night before, I felt surprisingly rested and alert. Absent were the stomach fits and heart palpitations I usually experienced when I had to confront my mother. I wasn't perspiring under my blouse, and my throat was free of lumps. All in all, I was stronger than I'd been in quite a while.

She sat behind the desk, one hand resting on an oversized leather-bound ledger and the other wrapped around a quill.

"Am I interrupting?" I asked.

"Have a seat." As she put her work aside, I took the chair opposite her and crossed my legs, the pointy toes of my high-heeled shoes peeking out from under my long, form-fitting skirt. Her eyes rested on my scar, and she visibly shuddered.

"Mother, do you truly care about me?" I asked.

"Of course I do, Regina. In fact, when I was playing croquet yesterday, I met some people who may be of use to us. You see, everything I've ever done, everything I ever do, is for you. I don't want you to have to go through the hardships I had to. I want you to live in the grandest castle imaginable, where you will have servants at your beck and call and citizens at your feet, eager to please you in any way they can. I have no doubt you will someday be queen, the most powerful ruler in all the land."

I licked my lower lip. "That's why I'm ready to make a deal with you."

"What do you have on the table this time?" She lifted a brow.

I had to look my mother in the eye. It was said that as an ogre killed someone, its victim saw his or her own reflection in the ogre's eyes. The notion had always enticed me. Did it fill the victim with terror or peace?

I set my jaw and, holding my head high, aimed my gaze directly into my mother's beautiful, powerful eyes. I checked to ensure my posture was perfect and cleared my throat so my voice wouldn't crack. Unblinkingly, unflinchingly, I spoke:

"If you give Claire her heart back, I will do everything in my power to make your dream come true. I'll happily go to every party or ball to which we receive an invitation, and if for some reason we are not on the list, I will weasel my way in, like you did during King Xavier's masquerade ball." I paused, and as expected, she smirked at the memory. "I will dance with whomever you pair me with. I'll use exemplary manners, especially when in public. I'll happily wear the clothes you choose for me, and I'll even tolerate the shoes that are too small." On the desk was a platterful of pastries, and I pushed it out of my reach. "I'll watch what I eat until I'm as thin as you like, and never drink cider again so as not to become a drunkard like my grandfather. I will act the part of a lady. I will behave like nothing short of a future queen. Am I forgetting anything? If so, please tell me."

"You will not try to learn magic from anyone other than me," she added. "And you will not engage in secret rendezvous."

"Yes, of course, Mother."

She blinked. Inhaled. Exhaled. Tapped her quill on the open page of her ledger. Ate a cherry tart off the platter and licked her fingers. It seemed an eternity passed before she responded.

"Very well," she said, finally. "Go and fetch Claire."

"I have a better idea," I said, and I ran upstairs. I popped into my bedroom, where I grabbed a message I'd written and slid it into my jacket pocket. Next I stopped in my parents' chambers for the wooden box my mother kept in her top bureau drawer. A moment later, I returned to my mother's office and handed her the box.

Grinning, my mother stood. For the first time in a very long while, I believed she was genuinely pleased.

She opened the box and tilted her head as she lifted the object that had been nestled in its velvety folds. Claire's heart glowed red. Though I'd seen it before, it still made my pulse race faster.

Next she turned to the mirror hanging on the wall, and in it, we saw Claire sitting in her uncle's attic, her knees drawn up to her chest and her hair hanging in unkempt strands down her spine. She gazed bleary-eyed out of the small round window at the hills between her uncle's estate and ours.

"She might very well be a true friend. When she has this again," my mother said, indicating the heart in her hand, "you will know." She turned to face the mirror again. "Come to me, Claire," she said, speaking into the heart. In the looking glass, I saw Claire's lower lip quiver as she scrambled to her feet and started wending through the possessions of her deceased aunt and infant cousin on her way to the arched attic door. My mother placed the beating heart in the box on her desk and closed the lid. "Is that all, Regina?"

"I have two more requests," I said boldly.

"Don't allow yourself to become greedy." My mother crossed her hands across her chest, but I could tell she was curious. Besides, she hadn't said no—at least, not yet.

I pulled the scroll out of my pocket. "Will you pass this along to Claire, before you put her heart back? Tell her she must do what it says."

"Very well," my mother agreed, taking it from me. "And what, pray tell, is your second request?"

"May I also have a forgetting potion?" I asked.

My mother cocked an eyebrow. "There are several types of forgetting potions. Which are you seeking?" she asked, striding over to the enormous armoire. Its doors creaked as she opened them, revealing shelves and drawers and an assortment of glass jars, bottles, and vials.

"I need one to make me forget I ever knew someone who was once important to me, but ended up being a traitor."

"Yes, I have the perfect spell for that." She ran her finger along one of the drawers and then pulled it slowly open. She selected a vial not much bigger than a thimble.

Before handing it to me, she gave it a shake, and it glowed purplish blue for a second.

"Thank you, Mother." I turned on my high heels, and she placed her palm on my shoulder to stop me.

"Sometimes, Regina, forgetting is a blessing. Other times it is a curse," she said meaningfully.

My mother's words echoed in my head even ten minutes later as I leaned on the white split-rail fence and watched Jesse put the sidesaddle on Rocinante. The stable boy kept eyeing me nervously, probably expecting me to raise a fuss. But at the moment I was a veritable hornet's nest of emotions, and the style of saddle I'd be sitting upon made little difference to me. After he helped me up, he handed me the riding crop. "When shall I tell your mother you'll be home?" he asked.

"Soon enough," I replied, and I rode quickly away from the stable. We'd barely started, and already I was as breathless as if I'd been riding for hours on end. Instead of going through the forest, I opted to take the road so Rocinante could gallop, and he did. I closed my eyes as the wind fanned my face, feeling every minute movement of the horse as if his body were my own. When I opened my eyes, I saw the spires of the castle towering in the cloudy sky. We were quickly approaching the royal gardens, and Rocinante needed little guidance to return to the bridge. While he sipped from the royal stream, I picked the most perfect yellow rose I could find and sat on the edge of the bridge, my knees bent and ankles crossed. Above, white puffy clouds grew and morphed into shapes of crowns, dragons, and a horse with a particularly voluminous tail.

At any moment, my mother would return Claire's heart to her, and Claire would return to her former self, able to feel and able to love. Still, I would never be able to trust her again. I'd waited so long to have a true friend, and when I finally thought I'd found one in Claire, I'd been sorely mistaken. My mother had offered her a deal, and she'd accepted without consideration of whom she was consequently hurting. I didn't know what my future held, but I refused to have Claire Fairchild be a part of it.

It would be easy for her to go home to Port Bennett, but I wanted her to be even farther away.

I slipped the vial out of my pocket and shook it, watching the potion glow. Rocinante lifted his head from the stream. He blew air through his nostrils and stomped his front hoof.

"It's going to be all right, my friend," I said as I hitched him to a tree. "You have to trust me."

With that, I made my way on foot to the grand entrance of King Leopold and Queen Eva's castle.

A spindly man with hair as white as snow came to the door when I rang the chimes. "Who shall I say has come to pay him a visit?" he droned.

"Regina. He's not expecting me, but I'm sure he'll be glad to see me."

"Very well. Please, come in. Would you like any refreshment whilst you wait?"

"Yes, thank you," I said. "Have you any cider?"

His bushy eyebrows sprang up on his forehead. "Cider, m'lady?"

I entertained the idea of explaining where he might find such a beverage, but I refrained. "Silly me," I said. "I meant tea. May I wait for him in the library?"

"Of course." He rang a bell, and a female servant appeared as if out of thin air.

Soon I was left alone in the royal castle's luxurious library. I gasped out loud at the most expansive collection of books I'd ever seen, and in every other nook, candles and fresh flower arrangements abounded. Moments later, the female servant reappeared with the most delicious tea my taste buds had ever experienced, and with a curtsy, she vanished once again.

I almost fell out of my chair when a man's voice exclaimed, "Regina! What a surprise!" Rising to my feet, I brushed a section of hair that had fallen onto my forehead behind my ear.

Prince Benjamin's cheeks were extra ruddy, and I

couldn't help noticing his britches were skewed on his disproportionately slim hips. Even worse, his undergarments spilled out of the waistline of his pants, and his shirt was buttoned in a way that caused an unfortunate gap in line with his hairy navel. A cursory glance out into the hallway, and at the equally flushed and disheveled maiden who fled past, clued me in to the nature of his prior engagement, and I felt a wave of pity for her.

"Hello, Benjamin," I said, holding up my teacup. "If you don't mind my saying so, you look thirsty. Perhaps you should have a drink."

"What a good idea," he said, and he stuck his head into the hall. Only moments after we'd both taken our seats, a young male servant appeared with an amber-colored beverage for the king and queen's special guest.

I gazed at Benjamin through my lashes. "Ever since the royal ball, I haven't been able to stop thinking about you."

"Go on," he said.

I swallowed my disgust and beamed at him. "My

father said you two played a lovely game of chess at our house."

Benjamin quaffed his drink. "I have the utmost respect for your father; however, he has a thing or two to learn about the game of chess."

"Perhaps if you and I begin courting, you can teach him," I said.

"So, you're considering my offer?"

I rose and wandered to the bookshelf. "How could I refuse?" I flashed him another smile and then pretended to be immersed in the various books.

"I didn't think you'd be able to," he agreed, and before I knew it, he was standing behind me, his alcohol-tinged breath wrapping around my head and into my nose.

"Especially since we have so much in common. Our love of books, for instance. Oh! I have a wonderful idea. Will you read me a passage?" I thrust a random novel into his hands. "This is one of my favorites," I said, tapping its leather cover. "I find it quite romantic."

Benjamin's face lit up. "Of course, my darling." He

cleared his throat and began flipping pages, apparently searching for a worthwhile chapter.

While he read, I circled around to the sitting area and stealthily poured the forgetting potion into his glass. As soon as he stumbled on a word above his aptitude, I invited him to drink more. And drink more he did.

Meanwhile, I watched his every move, hoping for a sign that the spell was taking effect. After two more sips, he began to sway. His head bobbled as if it weighed too much for his neck and his arms dangled limply at his sides. When the book fell to the floor, he made a sad whimpering noise.

"Hello," I said.

"Hello?"

"Are you all right, Prince Benjamin?"

"Are you speaking to me?"

Nodding, I led him back to his chair. "You fell and hit your head, and I'm afraid it might be affecting your memory."

"Who are you?" he asked.

"Oh, no," I said, sitting opposite him. "This is quite a mess. I'm your betrothed's closest friend. She wanted us to meet so that she can plan the most extravagant wedding the Enchanted Forest has ever seen. When you proposed to her, she agreed to move across the entire realm to be your wife."

"Oh?" He ran his fingers through his tufts of hair.

I nodded. "It's true."

"And this woman to whom I'm engaged? Who is she?"

"Goodness! You don't recall her name? This is a bigger mess than I thought."

He leaned forward and grasped my hands. "Please. Tell me her name. Tell me all about her. I don't want to offend or hurt my beloved, whoever she may be. I beg of you: tell me each and every detail."

"Very well," I agreed. "I can do that." As I told Claire's future husband about how she liked cider, riding horses, waltzing, and baked goods, I pictured in my mind's eye the note I'd left for Claire to read, back when she was still under my mother's control.

Dear Claire,

You are to wed Prince Benjamin on the twenty-fourth day of June. This is your wedding gift.

The friend you could have had,

Regina